LOVE LIES BLEEDING

By
Robert K. Swisher, Jr.

Contemporary Life Fiction Series

Sunstone Press · *Santa Fe* · *New Mexico*

All of the characters in this book
are fictitious, and any resemblance
to actual persons, living or dead,
is purely coincidental.

For the Madonna of the Truck Stop . . .Bless You . . .

First Edition

Printed in the United States of America

Library of Congress Cataloging in Publication Data:

Swisher, Jr., Robert K., 1947-
    Love lies bleeding / by Robert K. Swisher, Jr. -- 1st ed.
        p.   cm. -- (Contemporary life fiction series)
    ISBN: 0-86534-121-4 : $8.95
    I. Title. II. Series
    PS3569.W574L68   1989
    813'.54--dc19   88-2095
                                                                  CIP

Published in 1989 by SUNSTONE PRESS
                Post Office Box 2321
                Santa Fe, NM 87504-2321 / USA

CHAPTER I

They had all told me I would end up here one day. "They" being my folks and friends. Aunts and uncles, not being close enough blood, didn't have to formulate an opinion on where I would end up. But parents have to. They would look at me and shake their heads and I could see pain and lost hope in their eyes and they would tell me in many different ways how they couldn't understand and for sure I was headed for jail. Even when I was young, I knew they were right. I didn't fit into all the corners of young life. I didn't like Little League, I didn't like football or think about fucking all the girls. I spent a lot of time alone. That was the problem. I spent a lot of time alone thinking. That can be bad for you, thinking. It makes you wonder and not accept, and not accepting can get you in jail.

My grandmother was never like the rest of them, the caring people who had lost hope. She never looked away from me when she spoke or hid behind words. She always told me what she felt. And she loved me. Why I have never really understood but you know when somebody loves you. It's a bridge of pain between two people. Your hearts talk, not your mouths. It's all in the heart. Grandma would look at me and put her bent and twisted arthritic hand on my shoulder and just smile. And with that smile I knew she understood. It was okay to be different. It was tough but it was okay. I had a cornerstone with life in her. A place, no matter where I was, I could reach for with my mind and feel warm and safe. Even during the war I was safe. Even now that she was dead I could reach for that cornerstone. There may not be a God but there was love, somewhere in all the vast emptiness of universe there was my grandmother.

My grandmother died in the winter. The day we buried her it was six degrees and the snow was blowing off of the snow banks the plows left, making a road into the cemetery. There were many faceless people there. Old people bundled up with heavy coats and gloves and scarves around their faces. Bundled up enough you could not tell they were old but could have been young children out to make snowmen and throw snowballs. Many of the women, when they passed me, had tears frozen on their faces. Several of the men too. The sky was dull grey although it was early afternoon and the giant oak trees were a dull brown. I thought it was a shame for my grandmother to die in the winter and have to be buried in the cold. She deserved the summer, summer with all the greens and flowers blooming and the bees buzzing. But it was ironic, the brown lifeless oak trees matched the dull grey sky. I was happy for one thing. I was on trial then and she would never have to know.

I have been back to the cemetery once over the past years. Stood on a warm summer day when the breeze was blowing and the bees were buzzing and the gardener was watering the multicolored flowers. I stood and looked at the ground and the hump of lush green grass but all I could see was the snow and the old people who looked like children and her twisted pained hands reaching for me and telling me, "It's okay. It's hard but it's okay."

The past couple of years haven't been that bad. You get used to sitting in a five foot by twelve foot cell. You get used to watching your cellmate go to the bathroom in the toilet in the corner and listening to him jack off late at night. You get used to the ring of the clanging steel bars as the doors close and the holler of guards when the doors are about to be opened and you can go out to eat or to the TV room. You get used to the smell of men all crammed into small boxes. You get used to it all. That's what life is, getting used to, getting use to it so you can go on. But you learn, you learn a lot of things not really worth learning but you learn. You learn how to move through a day with your mind somewhere else. You learn to keep your mouth shut. You learn how to sharpen a spoon or make sure you always have a pen or pencil in your pocket in case you have to stab somebody. You learn how to read books through all the noise and how to write letters. Most of all you learn how to dream. You learn how to put yourself wherever you want to be. Fishing by some lake, making love to some pretty lady on a bed that is soft, driving a car, walking along a fence line and watching rabbits bounce away. But most of all you learn there really isn't any justice. No matter how long you have tried to convince yourself there is an order to life, a purpose, a reason, you learn that simply isn't true. There is no reason. But you still seek an order, a reason. It becomes one's life. To find something that is real. And you learn how to be a better criminal and how to hate. How to hate the guy who is doing your girlfriend. How to hate the warden, the hacks, the stool pigeons and other criminals. Prison is not a very nice place but it is real. And believe me, nobody is immune from prison. The people who make the laws change them all the time.

The prisons need you.

I was sent to prison for smoking marijuana. Seven years. I'm not bitter. I just shake my head. There is nothing much to say. It was like the first time I saw a man killed. He was walking and then there was a loud explosion and dirt flying everywhere. I didn't hit the ground that time. From then on I did but not that time. I stood and watched as the man's body went in different directions. A foot, an arm, a piece of face. All hurling through the air like they were entities of their own, not realizing everything was dead. After the explosion there was nothing to say. Not, "Oh shit," or "Fuck," or "Our Father." There was nothing. I remember it was quiet, the deepest quiet I have ever experienced in my life. Battle is like that. Loud, noisy, insane and when it is over the most profound quiet. The quiet of sinners. Nobody is right, not either side. That's why the quiet. Like shaking your head for getting seven years for smoking pot.

When I first walked into the penitentiary I found I wasn't really afraid. I don't know if I've ever really been afraid since the army. I had enough fear in the army to last more than this lifetime. I wasn't really afraid but I was sweating nervously. When the steel bars clanged shut behind me I knew for sure this was the place. But even standing inside the pen I didn't feel like a criminal. After being sprayed for bugs, my head shaved, I was locked in a small cell by myself. I stayed there thrity days. Thirty days of not leaving the cell except to eat. If you had money when you came in the joint you could go to the store once a week. Buy cigarettes, candy bars, evelopes, paper. If you didn't have money, well tough. Nothing different about the pen than on the outside. The pen reinforces the fact of no justice. After thirty days I was sent to the regular populace and started work in the store. Since I could read and write I worked in the store. And I was assigned to a cell with another man. He told me in time he had killed four people. I never asked him why. He just told me on Christmas. I told him I didn't really give a fuck what he had done. He said he didn't either. I gave him a cup of coffee and a cookie for Christmas. He had no family on the outside to send him money so he never got to buy things from the store. I had money so for shining my shoes and making sure my stuff didn't get stolen, I gave him things. Cigarettes, paper, coffee. It was worth it. Nobody tried to fuck with me and nobody stole my stuff. He used to sit on his bunk, the bottom one, Life sentence deserves the bottom bunk. He used to sit on his bunk and drink coffee and smoke and laugh. "You shouldn't be here for smoking pot, boy," he would say. "Shouldn't be here. Killers like me and rapers, sure, what the fuck? But pot? You shouldn't be here." I used to agree with him but after looking at the steel bars for a while it really didn't matter what one thought. Fact was, I was there. Facts are facts.

He and I talked about a lot of things over the last two years. Him lying on his bunk, me on mine. Staring into the grey cracked paint. Talked about taxes, love, Christmas. He always gave me a Christmas present, an apple he had stolen from the mess truck or an onion, or a pencil because he knew I wrote a lot. But we talked about a lot of things. Girls, children, war, hate, the law. It's strange but there I was with a few days left before my release and he was happy for me. "You write me now. Write me and tell me about the world and don't ever come back." I had already given him all my things. Typewriter, paper, bags of coffee, cigarettes. He would be rich for a while and then he would be somebody else's bodyguard. Years down the road I would be on the outside and he would still be there. Lying on the bunk talking to somebody about girls and taxes and life. Until one day he will die in that hole smelling of men and pain and they will bury him in the prison cemetery. "Good place for murderers," he said but it was still sad. Sad for him and sad for us that it all had to come about. No justice.

It will be scary to walk out of here. Scary because nothing in my mind has really changed. I came into this prison always a little confused about the world and I'm still confused. It seems I've always been anxious and afraid of life. Not fear like fear of an enemy. More like fear of the dark. An anxious fear, trying to explain why the world isn't right. Too much promise for things to be the way they are. Watching men kill each other in a war, watching grey paint and birds through bars hasn't taken any of the confusion or fear or anxiety away. And now time is putting me back into the world. I don't have any money. I haven't finished college. I really don't know what I want·to do but I have to do something. For sure something is going to happen. The sun is going to come up and the sun is going to come down and I'm going to have to eat and sleep like everybody else. I hope I can find a girl. The one I had when I came in here is gone. Just as well, new start now. No going backwards, new dreams. Looking for love between sunup and sundown. Love seems to make it all a little easier. But exactly what I'm going to do I don't really know. I'd like to travel. Stick out my thumb and hit the road. West first, west to California and the warmth and the ocean. Feel the ocean breeze on my face and eat boiled shrimp and crab and look at pretty California ladies with their bikinis. Then maybe I'll head up the coast to Washington and across the top of America. I really don't know. Maybe it's just another dream. I've had so many over the past years it's hard to sort them out at times. But it's not long. Not long before the bars slam shut behind me and I am going to be standing on the street not looking back. It's OK, Grandma. It's not easy, but it's OK. I'll learn to believe. I did once. I'll learn again.

I got up as usual this morning at four AM. Brushed my teeth and combed my hair and waited for the bars to open to go eat breakfast. Stood in line with all the other men and ate in silence my scrambled eggs and toast. But this morning I looked closely at the men. Young men, old men, tired, restless faces. Tired of dreaming, tired of passing time. Lost men. I looked at the faded green paint of the mess hall and the stainless steel trays and at the hacks dressed in grey standing around the mess hall. And I thought to myself, this isn't worth remembering but I know I will remember it. Remember it like I remember the war and catching my first fish with my father and the first time I slept with a girl. At eight o'clock I shook hands with my cell mate and followed the hack to the door where I signed a few papers in front of the warden who shook my hand smiling. ''Don't want to ever see you again, boy,'' he muttered between cigar-stained teeth. ''We'll always be here, you know.'' I shook hands with him but said nothing. Nothing to say. Like blown-up people and no justice, nothing to say. Standing outside with my black shoes and red pants and blue shirt and three hundred dollars, I didn't feel free or happy. I didn't feel like jumping up or down or singing. I didn't want to climb to the top of a mountain and holler to the world I made it. All I know was it was spring and I was free. I walked to where the warden told me the bus station was and threw my discharge papers in the first garbage can I passed. Inside the bus station I looked around and it seemed the people waiting for buses had the same tired faces the men in the joint had. I bought a ticket for Albuquerque, New Mexico. I wanted out of Texas as fast as I could get out.

Sitting by a window on the bus I watched the trees and cars

roll by. I felt as though I had been on a long ship ride. Seeing the world through a porthole. Able to look out at the world but unable to reach out and touch anything. It just kept going by, port after port without ever letting me off. But here it was, the world. America, land of dreams, land of opportunity. Here it was and here I was with the thought in my head I was going to go see my country and try to find what I had lost. Years in the pen deserved a year on the road. I was free, as free as three hundred dollars minus a bus ticket and a cup of coffee could make me. Across the aisle an old man with no teeth and ragged clothes gnawed on a sandwich. In front of me two large black women in their mid-forties talked about knitting and behind me sitting on the large bench seat that ran along the back of the bus a young couple held hands and kissed each other. I was off of the ship, it was like getting back from the war, a bus ride and nobody noticed or cared.

I don't know where I was when the sun went down. I was looking out the window wondering if the lovers in the back of the bus were going to be brave during the night and suddenly it was dark. It felt good to sit in the dark. In the pen it was never dark. There are always lights on. You get used to it. But now it was dark and the dark was like an old friend. I knew there were people around me but like me the dark had made them silent and thoughtful. A time to rest and think, be truly alone. I sat and thought about my folks. I had not called them. They had never been to visit me in the pen. My father would have come but not my mother. I told them not to come. What for? Prove they had been right? Add to their shame and embarassment? But I thought of them. I thought of them at Christmas decorating the tree and my sister standing on tiptoe to reach the high branches. My brother and his wife herding their children around and all of them drinking hot cider and laughing. And all of them, in their own way, thinking of me. Not talking about me but thinking. That's the thing about families. Even in shame they are there. If I ever have a family, no matter what my children are, they will always be welcome at my house. That's what a family should be. A place where it is Christmas every day. A place where Sister stands on her tiptoes and little children run around not knowing of life and you can drink hot cider and laugh and forget about the world for a while. But I don't know if I can go home now. In time. Now it wouldn't be worth it. Nothing to say.

The bus stopped in some small Texas town for dinner. The lady behind the counter was big and cheerful. One of those ranch bred girls. Big arms, big breasts, big heart. You knew she could get up before the sun and cook for six men off to work on the land and be just as she was now, smiling, talking to everybody. She made me feel warm when she set the cup of coffee down on the counter. Everybody in a bus stop drinks coffee. You don't have to ask. She looked at my short hair and red pants and blue shirt and face without a tan and she knew where I had been. But she only smiled and said, "Chicken fried steak is the special," and added, "Try it, you'll like it." I noticed the small gold ring on her dishwater-chapped hand and then she was gone. She walked over to the two large black women sitting at the table and I could hear her jovial voice over the juke box the bus driver was playing. When she came back I told her I wanted the special. She brought me cole slaw first, good slaw, big chunks of cabbage dripping with dressing, slaw like you ate on a picnic under a shade tree during the summer. The steak overlapped the plate and the mashed potatoes covered half the steak. The corn was thrown over the top of it all. And it was good. Good greasy food, food that filled you up and made you able to work for hours. Food that in time put fat on your bones and two chins under your face. I ate it all and wiped the plate with a piece of of unbuttered white bread. Then I ate the peach pie she brought and drank another cup of coffee. She took the checks around to all the other people, all the time carrying on to the bus driver about how bad the weather had been this year. Not enough rain for a flea to get a drink. But when she came to me she just walked on by, her large expanse of bottom swaying the blue cheap dress. The bus driver stood and took another sip of coffee and called, "Time to go, ladies and gentlemen." I stood reaching for my billfold and called, "Miss, I need my check." She walked over to me with a brown sack and set it on the counter. "Here's a piece of pie for you. Dinner's on me. Welcome home. Got me a brother down there now. He's not bad, just poor." I looked at the lady as big as Texas and lowered my head. "Thanks," I mumbled. "Thank you." She smiled pushing the brown lunch sack at me and I turned and walked out into the night and the dark insides of the bus. Strange, getting out of Nam nobody gave me anything. Getting out of prison a stranger gave me dinner.

The bus pulled off leaving behind a cloud of diesel smoke and the diner. I clutched the brown bag, the bottom of it resting on my leg and felt the heat from the pie on my leg. Staring out into the dark I wished I had said something to the woman. I didn't even know her name. I wished I could have hugged her and felt her large breasts against my chest and told her thank you, thank you for making me feel human.

Somewhere in a small town in Texas she is still there. Smiling to weary people who get off buses, talking about the weather to bus drivers with sore backs and not enough money. Working for tips that consist of quarters and dimes, not dollars like the fancy restaurants. But it's all relative. Then after work she takes off her apron and goes home. Home to some small farmhouse to cook and clean and help her man with cattle and horses and kids. I think she must be always smiling. I would like to believe she is. The perpetual helper. The Madonna of the bus stop. Dear Lady, I hope all is well with you and yours.

About midnight I ate the pie and thought about the men at the pen sleeping. They were still on the ship. They weren't eating pie. They didn't feel human. But I didn't feel bad. That's how it is sometimes. It isn't always fair but that doesn't mean it's always bad.

Riding through the night, the sound of the big bus tires humming on the pavement, was a good feeling. Driving is like a time machine. There is no future really, just the endless highway that seems to unwind in front of you through the glare of the headlights. I thought about an old bum I had picked up beside the road in Kansas. I was sixteen years old and had spent the summer working on a ranch in Kansas. I hitchhiked out of El Paso to Delhart, Texas, and caught a ride with a combine crew to Syracuse, Kansas. There I got a job driving tractors. All summer long I drove around and around the biggest fields you have ever seen in your life, plowing up stubble from wheat crops. It was a good job. Day after day, around and around, eating dirt, getting rained on, drinking water from a burlap covered gallon jug and lunch from a sack the rancher's wife gave me. I got two hundred and fifty dollars a month and room and board. I was rich. I bought a pair of black boots, smoked cigarettes and chewed tobacco. What else was there to life? At the end of summer, coming back from Kansas, I had a '54 Pontiac with a flat head eight in it. It purred like a kitten. When I pulled into a rest stop I saw an old man sitting under a tree. He had a gunny sack stuffed with odds and ends beside him and was dressed in a mismatch of clothes. His face was covered with whiskers and a dirty brown hat was on his head. After relieving myself in the bathroom I walked back to the car and was about to get in when the old man called me. His voice was strong, which surprised me. "How about a ride, young'en?" I was a little afraid, I have never really seen a bum before. I thought they were only part of stories, not real. People weren't bums in America. I nodded my head OK and he rose slowly and walked over to the car putting his gunny sack between his legs in the front seat. Looking back now, I imagine he was as afraid of me as I was of him. When all you own is a gunny sack you really don't want it stolen. We drove in silence for a few miles and then I lit up a smoke. I offered him one, which he took gladly. He didn't say much, in fact he didn't say anything. I offered him some chicken the rancher's wife had fried for me for the ride home and he ate it like a starving dog. I think if I hadn't been there he would have eaten the bones. I let him eat it all and even the chocolate cake, which to this day I have never eaten any better. After eating he smoked another cigarette I gave him. By then even his smell didn't bother me. When it got dark he stared to talk. More like talking to himself. The dark makes one do that. He had been a sergeant in the army during World War II. But after the army he worked all kinds of jobs. Combine crews, beet picker, watermelons down in Texas. Did a little bit of everything. But now he was too old and was heading for Arizona where it was warm and he could live off of oranges and grapefruit during the winter. Then he became silent. I kept looking over at the old man and his eyes were open. He sat as though he was not alive. Just sat unmoving with his sack between his legs, looking out the window into the darkness. Every time I looked over at him he had still not moved. Then, with him forgotten and I in my own thoughts, he spoke, "How about we heat up a can of soup?"

"How?" I asked.

"Pull the car over."

I pulled over, being young and used to being told what to do and he rummaged around in his sack and pulled out a can of chicken noodle soup.

"Pop the hood," he ordered.

I popped the hood and he got out, I got out and he set the can of soup on the engine. Shutting the hood he got back into the car. I drove off and about fifteen minutes later he said simply, "Soup's done." We stopped and I opened the hood and he took the can of soup, opened it and the soup was warm. A few hours later the road divided and I let him out. I can still see the old man standing by the road putting the pack of cigarettes I gave him into his tattered jacket pocket with his gunny sack by his leg and his brown hat rumpled on his head. And I can still smell the soup in the old '54 Pontiac as we passed the can back and forth without talking. It was the only way the old man had of paying me for the chicken and the cake, sharing his can of soup. He only took the cigarettes because I told him I was quitting. You think about funny things when you're riding a bus at night, full of chicken fried steak and feeling human.

At five AM the bus stopped. The driver muttered something about New Mexico and got out. The other people slept but I got out and looked at the eastern sky turning a pale crimson. It was grand. I took deep breaths and stomped my feet. Inside the bus stop I sat next to the bus driver and drank coffee and ate a sweet roll. He was a thin man, taller than most men and said little. Years of driving a bus can make a man say little. It was just as well. I didn't have much to say either. A day out of the pen it was OK. I was out of Texas. I felt the pat of my grandmother's hand on my shoulder. "It isn't easy but it's OK, Grandma," I spoke to myself and walked outside the station and watched the sun with all its glory rise above the horizon and bathe the land with a golden kiss. You can believe in the sun. The sun will never let you down.

CHAPTER II

I spent a week in Albuquerque. The first night I spent in a cheap hotel listening through the paper-thin walls to the passion of what must have been a clandestine love affair. Married couples, after a few years, no longer seem to have the amount of passion that emitted from the other room. The next day I bought several pairs of levis, some white western shirts, a pair of brown cowboy boots, a levi jacket and a suitcase to hold my things. I chucked the prison clothes in a Goodwill box. That night I splurged and rented a room at the Hilton. Soaked in a Jacuzzi until I was a prune. Had shrimp for dinner and several drinks at the bar. The next three days I worked at a truck stop washing down trucks with three wet-backs. Since I can't speak Spanish or they English, we spent the days smiling at each other and more or less keeping out of each other's way. They were good workers. I slept in the truck stop and they slept in a row of bushes behind the truck stop. My fortune once again up to three hundred dollars. I walked to the freeway in my new clothes and stuck out my thumb. It was a beautiful spring day. The New Mexico sky was a deep blue, as if someone had thrown the ocean from around a coral reef up into the air. By ten in the morning my happiness was still undampened. Getting out of prision has a way of making everything look up no matter how bad it gets. Something to do with freedom. Taken for granted by many people in this country. But try losing it for a while. Check yourself into the joint for a few weeks if you need a refresher course.

A little past ten a Volkswagen bus slowed to a stop before me. The once blue and white was now blue and white on rust with two tires I could see were running on prayer and I imagine the other two were just as bad. A faded pink plastic flower long beyond recognition dangled from the antenna. I opened the door and the driver blurted between his long free flowing beard dotted with white, "Jump in, friend." His hair was pulled back and the rubber-banded pony tail disappeared between his back and the seat. His shirt was patched many times and his jeans had several holes in them. The boots he was wearing seemed in good shape. I glanced in the back after shutting the door. On a mattress where the seats used to be, under blankets so only their faces and one foot stuck out, were two women.

"Jesus Christ," I blurted out. "I didn't know hippies still survived."

The man laughed a deep geniune laugh. "I wonder at times myself," he answered. "Maybe we're just floating souls of THC and what used to be bodies have long gone the way of. . . " Here he paused and added in a monent, "Where ever old hippies go." I hadn't thought of hippies in years. I had been one and it seemed like centuries ago. "Those two girls in the back, I picked them up on the other side of the state." He spoke nodding towards the back. "One on the left gives great head. Her name is Sue. One on the right doesn't talk much. Sue told me her boyfriend just ran off with some little sweet thing from Florida and left her nothing. Men and women," he laughed. "Same old shit. Rich people, poor people, in between people. When it come to men and women, it's the same old shit."

I had a monentary fleeting pain over my last love but I smiled at his wisdom. The bearded one held out his hand. "Jim. Jim's my name. Headed for California and home."

I decided he looked like Yosemite Sam as I shook his hand. "Frank," I told him.

He eyed me thoughtfully. "Ever think, Cowboy, you'd be riding with a hippy?"

I laughed before answering. "Used to be a hippy myself but it's a long story."

Jim laughed louder and harder than I did. "Funny," he finally blurted, "I used to be a cowboy." A few moments later as he was down shifting to get the wheezing Volkswagen over a slight hill he asked, "Got a joint?"

I shook my head. "No, quit smoking the stuff. Used to but not anymore." I didn't feel like telling him I just got out of prison for pot. What for?

Jim shrugged his shoulders. "Just asking. I ran out a few hundred miles ago. Guess I'll just have to make it."

We rode on in silence, the odor of patchouli oil coming from the back of the bus. Presently I heard the girls stirring and turning was surprised to see two of the loveliest blue eyes looking directly into mine. Sue still slept. The girl smiled deeply, exposing nice even teeth and when she said hello her small thin lips smiled slightly. "Hi," I answered. She moved out from underneath the covers and straightened as best she could her cowboy shirt. She was wearing well-faded jeans and she pulled on cowboy boots without socks. Her hair was long and flaxen. I could not take my eyes off of the woman. She was too old to be a girl. When she was done straightening and putting on her boots, she spoke with no malice in her voice, "Like what you see?"

I turned away and faced the highway. "Sorry," I spoke, feeling my neck turn red. "Nothing wrong intended." But then I added. "Yeah, you're pretty. I haven't seen a pretty lady in a while."

She stuck her head between Jim and me and said, "Listen, didn't mean to make you feel bad." And then she sat back down on the mattress. "Thanks for thinking I'm pretty." I could see a slight look of disgust on Jim's face. One of those looks that says,

"Asshole, it's people like you that ruin all the women for the rest of us."

"My name is Barbara. What's yours?"

Jim blurted in. "Frank. His name is Frank."

"I'm not talking to you, hairbrain," Barbara snapped.

Jim retorted, "You want out right now?"

"If you want, jerk," she shot back. But Jim did not stop, probably harboring in the back of his mind the question if she gave as good of head as Sue. "Well, Frank," Barbara went on. "Nice to meet you." She then rummaged around in the back and found a small suitcase and opening it took a brush out and began to brush her hair.

My heart was pounding and my mouth felt dry. I noticed in the mirror the outline of her small breasts against her shirt as she brushed her hair. I felt myself falling into some deep dark hole where all reason would leave me and all course of direction I had thought out over the past year would be gone.

Jim pulled the bus into a rest area and I got out. Barbara crawled over Sue and stood to stretch. "It's a lovely day," she spoke. I nodded at her and walked to the rest room. Jim was already inside brushing his teeth and splashing water onto his face. He spit out toothpaste and looked at me, winking. "You can have her. I was goin to try and fuck her this evening but you can have her. She likes you. I can tell." I felt like saying thank you but didn't.

Back outside Barbara was sitting on a concrete picnic bench. She had washed her face. I noticed she was at the most thirty and lovely. "Where are you going?" she asked.

I noticed the sun glisten off her golden hair and how her eyebrows were almost invisible. "California," I answered simply.

"Why?"

I felt ill at ease, not having talked to women for several years.

"Sit up here," she told me patting the table beside her. I immediately obeyed, weak man that I am, and sat beside her and for the first time smelled her perfume. I almost fainted. "Why?" she repeated.

"I don't know," I answered, regaining my thoughts. "Time in my life to see the country a little, is all."

"What are you looking for, Frank?" she asked sincerely, as if she knew me.

I stood up feeling cornered and looked away from her to a lone tree across the road in the other rest area. "I'm looking for me," came simply to my lips as I turned. Then I walked away feeling stupid.

She ran to my side and took my hand laughing. "Don't walk away." I looked at her as she still held my hand and she started to walk, more or less leading me until I was walking beside her. We walked around the rest area and then out behind where volcanic rock was between small pinon trees. We did not speak but looked at scampering lizards and chattering chipmunks fighting over a Frito and the darting sparrows in front of us. Back at the picnic table she smiled, "You can talk to me. It's okay, Frank."

I looked at her and with the blue New Mexico sky and the chipmunk and sparrows I felt a bent and withered hand reached out from the heavens and touch my shoulder, patting me. It was okay. I smiled faintly at the stranger. I drank of her eyes and her lips and her smile and I spoke softly, "Thank you."

"Well, if you two are tired of fucking around, we can leave," Jim spoke walking up to us. He sounded angry but you could tell he wasn't. He just needed more pot. Sue came bouncing out of the rest room and walked over to us. "Well hello, handsome," she spoke to me and giggled. Jim ran his hand over his pony tail. "I was driving my bus peacefully to California and now I've put myself in the situation of having company."

"You need gas," Barbara answered. "If you had money you wouldn't have picked any of us up."

Sue ran her tongue over her lips. "Us maybe but not the cowboy."

We piled back into the bus, women in the back and men in the front, and started once again west. I looked at the passing landscapes but my mind was still on the rest area and the chipmunks and wondering why I felt at ease with Barbara.

The next stop was Gallup, New Mexico. I bought gas and looked at the cheap Indian trinkets for sale in the gas station. Jim fiddled some with the engine. Sue and Barbara drank a coke. Back on the road we drove through Indian land. Along the highway there were scattered houses surrounded by poverty. I wondered what happened to the old Indian gods now that the white man ran the land. I wondered if they had traveled to another planet or if they were just holed up in the mountains somewhere waiting for another time. An hour before the sun set Jim pulled off the freeway and drove down a dirt road for a few miles. We spent some time gathering dried wood from the sparse juniper trees and as the sun went down we sat around a small fire watching Jim's coffee pot boil and eating Fritos and bean dip Sue had bought at the last stop. Presently Jim went to the bus and threw several blankets out on the ground and he and Sue, without a good night, got into the bus and shut the sliding door. Barbara sat across the fire from me sipping coffee. It was beautiful. Not cold, not hot. The stars were out by the thousands. I gazed into the fire and remembered when I was a little boy and my father took me on my first deer hunt. I don't remember how old I was exactly, eight or nine, but I remember the fire. I had sat there listening to the men talk. They talked about war and old girl friends and told off-color jokes, laughing and farting. I had not said anything, not wanting to ruin my welcome, not being a part of the grownup world yet.

I sat listening and looking into the fire. It was peaceful, filled with mystery and time. Barbara stood. "You don't have a sleeping bag?" I shook my head no. "We can share the blankets, but I'm not like Sue, okay?" She walked over and got the blankets and put one on the ground and the other at the end of it. "Come on over, " she spoke. I stood and sat down beside her. We both sat gazing at the fire without speaking.

"You don't talk much, do you?" she spoke presently.

I smiled faintly. "Not usually."

"Me either. Most talk is just a bunch of words thrown out at people to convince other people of how good we are. It's like the world is one great big bar and we sit around half-drunk talking about nothing and thinking people understand us over the blaring music."

I half-laughed but then the serious side of me came through. "People have to talk. Not all talk is useless." Barbara put a branch on the fire. "Talk is all we have with other people," I continued. "Talking is the pathway to our hearts."

Barbara lay down on the blanket. Before shutting her eyes she spoke. "I like you, Frank." And then just as quickly she was asleep.

I sat looking at the flames as they died down, warmed by them and the presence of a pretty lady, and I remembered when I was a hippy. It felt strange now but it was true, at one time I could have been called a hippy.

The war was over for me in '67. I was home and back in college. Ideals were shattered and things I had held for true were not. So I let my hair grow, started smoking pot and moved to the mountains.

It had been good in the mountains. There were many of us, smoking pot, loving, playing music, talking of the right world. A world filled with love and sharing. It didn't last long. How could it? We were children of the pampered age. And the world doesn't pamper. It teaches with slaps and punches, not kisses. I guess I really wasn't a hippy. Hard to become a hippy after the infantry but it was fun to play and grow vegetables and eat acid and dream after the war. It wasn't any big thing, really. The government made it a big thing. I still feel that they should have ignored the freaks and they would have drifted off into space on their own accord. There still are people like Jim scattered around the country. Still believeing in peace and long hair and beads. Trying to hold out with no money or insurance or nice clothes. But that's all they're doing. Holding out or hanging on. Not willing to give up or not able. That's how it is with beliefs. You hold onto them for so long that even when they are proven wrong, you can't let go. Too much of your life is used up trying to still believe. It's like losing a lover. It's hard to let go when you know you should. The hippies, they were going to change the world. Peace and love. They learned. You can't beat the system. The system just goes on and on, changing into another system but still a system. Based on power and greed but telling you it's for glory and the honor it possesses. But it was fun. Fun and fleeting and it did make some changes. Jane Fonda became famous. Bob Dylan built a big house in Malibu. Joan Baez got rich. Cowboys even grew their hair long. The world smoked pot. You don't see peace symbols anymore or beaded necklaces. I know a few old hippies. They have good jobs and their kids are in high school. Their wives have diamond rings and designer clothes. They drive Volvos and other foreign cars. And still deep in their hearts they are mad at America. They have become what they were against. The system wins. Even revolution is just another system.

I lay back down on the blanket and covered Barbara and me up. In the dim glow of the fire I looked at her face and wondered what she would think if she knew she was sleeping next to a convict. As I lay covered by the blanket next to Barbara with the stars as our ceiling, I felt small and afraid, a creature searching for himself and for somebody to love and be with. Somebody to say to, "Look at that tree," or "Look at that star." I looked once more at Barbara's sleeping form and told her unhearing ear, "Tonight, pretty lady, I share with you the stars." And I fell quietly and comfortably asleep.

In the morning I awoke with the horizon turning purple. Barbara had her arm over my chest and her hair covered my chin. I kissed her tenderly on the forehead just to remember what it felt like to be tender. I wondered what moment in time brought me to be with a woman lying on a blanket under the fading stars. Life is divided into very small moments that take on meaning. I lay still, not wanting to wake Barbara or take the moment away forever.

When the sun was up completely. Barbara woke up, She was not startled by her arm over me and turned her head slightly and kissed me on the cheek before sitting up. The sunrise was lovely framed by the back of her head with her blond hair cascading down her back.

When Jim and Sue rolled out of the bus we picked up the gear and drove to the rest area to clean up once again. I felt relaxed. The world was at peace for the moment.

Before we climbed back into the bus Barbara told me, "It was nice sleeping by you last night."

For most of the day we drove in silence. Late in the afternoon Jim felt like talking. Sue was sleeping and Barbara was reading. I looked out the window and thought about Barbara. I felt good but could not define the feeling. Jim started. "You said you were a hippy once. What happened?"

"I don't know really," I replied. "Time, maybe I never really believed in it all. Maybe it was only a dream, peace and all." I didn't want to tell Jim I had been in Vietnam. I had enough of telling people about it. It was another one of those no-need-to-talk subjects. Everybody had his own opinion and that was enough. It was like talking about God. Even God must be tired of the conversation.

"What were you, in the army or something?" Jim asked.

I rubbed my head. "Yeah, I was in the army." Jim nodded his head as though he knew all along but then dropped the subject to my relief.

"Hippies were kind of a funny thing," Jim went on. "It was like something went over the earth for a while and dropped a bit of consciousness on a handful of people. We ran around and believed in some unattainable cause and burnt up all the consciousness and then drifted back into the world." Jim looked over at me and there was almost pleading in his voice. "Do you think we did anything?"

I took a deep breath. "Yeah, we filled a lot of jails with drug cases and stopped a war I suppose."

"Kind of like those ruins you see of ancient people," Jim lamented. "You wonder what they did, how they lived, what they believed in. But they're gone now. Everything they did is gone except for some relics." Jim rubbed his head. "Guess I'm an old relic." With that the conversation ended. I felt sorry for Jim for a while. Sorry for Jim and Sue. Holding on to each other for a dead belief. But the feeling passed quickly. I feel sorry for myself sometimes and it also passes. If feeling sorry for oneself can pass, it sure can pass for others.

That night we stopped in the desert not far from the California line. It was warm and we ate fruit bought in the last town. There was no need for a fire. Once again Jim and Sue headed for the bus. Barbara smiled at me and asked if I wanted to go for a walk.

Barbara took my hand. The stars were bright and the desert quiet. We walked and did not speak. There was a magic with the night. Magic when you are with one and do not have to speak. You share something in the heart. A soundless music that brings you together. Magic spreads from fingertip to fingertip bringing your bodies and minds into one. I stopped walking and held Barbara's hand up to my lips and kissed the back of her hand. Then I pulled her close to me. I will never forget this night, Barbara in my arms, the stars and desert around us. There was no other world. No freeway, no bus, no prisons, no old wars, no need. Only two people holding each other without speaking.

That night we lay once again in each other's arms and slept. I did not dream.

Late the next afternoon we started down the hill from Barstow towards L.A. The grey green smog spread before us covering the city like the ocean covering the legendary Atlantis. It was a depressing sight. I wished I could put on air tanks and a mask but like everybody else we drove into the ooze and forgot it. Another thing you learn in life. You just forget it. You know it won't go away but if you forget it, then it's okay. Everybody is going to die anyway so just forget it. I hadn't seen city freeway traffic in years. It's always a fascinating sight. Suddenly there you are zipping along with the rest of humanity, looking out the window and wondering where in the hell everybody is going. But then, they're probably wondering where in the hell you are going also.

Somewhere on Sepulvada Boulevard Jim stopped. "Well, this is it, folks. End of the line."

I got out of the car as did Barbara. Sue crawled over the front seat and sat down. "Good luck," Sue spoke through the window and the Volkswagen bus was gone throwing out a small dark cloud as Jim accelerated to add to the soup of the air. I looked around me feeling lost. It's one thing to be in the mountains or desert with no where to go but another to be in the heart of a city.

Barbara must have felt my confusion as she asked. "Do you know where you are going?" I shrugged my shoulders and shook my head no. "Well, come with me then." We walked several blocks. I was feeling like a foreigner looking at the cars and people. Barbara hailed a cab and before I knew it we were once again on the freeway and in the traffic. Barbara sat unspeaking looking out the window. I felt like her child. The cab took us to Venice Beach and stopped in front of a two story house with white stairs that went to the top floor. Barbara paid the cab driver and started walking up the stairs. I hesitated at the bottom looking at the small section of beach I could see between the buildings. "It's okay," she coaxed. "The upstairs is my place. My folks gave it to me."

There was a small kitchen, a small living room and on either side of the bathroom two small bedrooms. Plants hung in front of all the windows and the furniture was the kind you buy in Mexico. "You can stay in that room." Barbara said as she pointed to the room on the left of the bathroom. I went inside and set my suitcase down and looked around. There was a mattress on the floor covered with a blanket that had a unicorn on it and a desk with a reading light. It was a nice room. The sun was shining through the window and the two hanging ivy plants gave it a feeling of being bigger than it was. I heard Barbara rustling around in her room and I went out and sat in the living room. She came out dressed in a white bikini and had a beach towel thrown over her shoulder.

"Ever see the ocean?" she grinned.

"Not in a long time."

"Got any swimming trunks?"

"No."

She went back into her room and returned with a pair of blue boxer trunks. "Put these on." I knew better than to ask whose they were. We strolled down to the ocean with her in the bikini and flip flops and me in boxer trunks and cowboy boots. I took my boots off once on the beach. She laid out the towel and immediately ran to the water and dove in. On the horizon large tankers moved slowly by with a sailboat closer to shore. Windsurfers passed like small flights of butterflies. Barbara waved at me as she splashed in the ocean like some happy puppy. I ran and jumped in head first and froze. I ran back as fast as I could and stood shivering. Barbara giggled. "You get used to it." I felt like saying, "You get used to it but your nuts won't," but I didn't. I went back and wrapped the towel around me and watched the various people stroll by. I gazed at the ships and the seemingly endless horizon of ocean. It was a strange but wonderful feeling. I had forgotten about the soupy air and the traffic. There was nothing but ocean going on forever. I thought to myself. How odd. Here I am sitting by the ocean and back in Texas there are people sitting in cells dreaming of this. The concept of different realities has always baffled me. At that moment I was highly baffled and cold.

Barbara ran up and flopped down on the sand. Goose bumps covered her body and I could not help but look at the goose bumps on the top of her breasts. She shut her eyes and sighed. "I love the ocean." I wanted to tell her of all the nights I lay on my bunk dreaming of the ocean. Dreaming of some girl in a bikini sitting beside me. And here right at this moment the dream was coming true. She lay on the sand and I sat until my skin was no longer blue and then we walked back to her house as the sun was sinking into the ocean. I had seen the sun set upon the water seventeen times in my life. On a troop ship headed for Nam. Each time it was like a miracle. There was no definition, no space. The sun just starts to sink and you feel as though great billows of steam should erupt around it. Then it is gone and the stars are out. But I had never seen it with a girl. As I stood on her porch I almost felt like crying. It was too good to be true.

Inside, Barbara still in her swim suit, put water on to boil for instant coffee. "Tell you what," she said. "Since you seem to be lost, I'll take you to dinner tonight. You shower first. It will take me longer."

Taking a shower was a delight. There were small bars of scented soap, sponges, hair rinses, and flowers stuck to the walls. All the little female touches. The towel was deep and soft and to my delight there was not a man's razor in the medicine cabinet, nor cologne or after shave. Dressed in clean levis and shirt, I went back to the living room. Barbara poured coffee and we sat at the small table under the kitchen window. It was dark outside and she turned on a light in the kitchen.

"I'm really thankful for this," I spoke. "I'll pay you."

"Sure," Barbara agreed. "But it's no problem. I can use the company." We drank the coffee and I looked around as one does when in a new place. Barbara stood and walked by. "I'll get ready." I watched her fanny and the gentle curve of her shoulder blades. Hearing the water come on in the shower, I thought, "We used the same soap. The soap I used on my body is now running over hers." I tried to visualize her standing naked under the spray of water with white rivulets of soap running over her nipples and gliding gently down through her pubic hair, running down her long legs to go down the drain. I ached to be the soap. I stood up from the table and went out to the porch. The steady hum of traffic filled the night mixed with the salt smell of the ocean. Miles and miles of water, filled with little snails, fish, squids and whales and one celled animals. Millions upon millions of forms of life all traveling along, pushed and pulled by the great currents and not caring where they are going or what they are doing. Not filled with shame or hurt or pain or needing love. Just living and being what they were. I wished I was some organism in the ocean and not Frank standing on a porch in LA surrounded by millions of people I did not know and going to have to be something or die broke and lonely in some VA hospital, "Dear Lord," I thought. "Even prison hasn't taught me what I should be. Thirty-five years and I just might as well be twelve again." I went back inside and refilled my coffee cup. The shower was turned off but the bathroom door was still closed. I could imagine Barbara running the soft towel over her body and I decided it was better for me to go back to the porch and think about the ocean.

Back on the porch I thought about being a kid in high school and everybody was talking about what they wanted to be when they grew up. Some wanted to be dentists. Others doctors, lawyers, race car drivers, football players and baseball stars. I went to army recruiting meetings and college introduction classes. But there was nothing I wanted to be. I had wanted to be a cowboy a hundred years ago or a scout for a wagon train or a fighter pilot during World War II. My girl friend at the time used to tell me, "You have to decide what you want to do." I would never ask her why because it made me feel more stupid but I wondered why. I guess I thought it would just come to me one day. One day I would be lost and the next day I would be found and it would all be okay. But the day never came. One night as I tried to get my hand under her blouse I told her I just wanted to live and see the world. She immediately removed my hand and told me I couldn't just live and see the world. I asked why and she told me a truth in life I will always remember. "Cause you're not rich, that's why." I decided that night back at my home I would be rich but it is difficult to get rich when one doesn't know what he wants to do.

The door opened and Barbara stepped out and stood beside me. "Relaxing?" she asked.

"Just thinking," I answered.

"Well, thinker, are you ready?"

We went back inside and I saw she wore a pale blue dress cut low in the front with the hem hitting her at the knees. She had on brown sandals and had painted her toenails a light pink. I told her she was pretty. She smiled and did a half curtsey saying, "Flattery will get you everywhere." We walked up the slight incline of the road and turned left. On the corner was a small Chinese restaurant. Inside there were not more than fifteen tables with all but one empty. The Chinese waiter, grinning from ear to ear, escorted us to a table. Barbara ordered a strawberry daiquiri and I the same. They were delicious. Eating sweet and sour pork and fried rice, I wondered where was the girl I had been going with before I went to prison. It was a passing moment. A moment of comparison for what I felt brewing in my heart for Barbara. I hoped she was fine wherever she was. Barbara, true to her word, picked up the check and as we were leaving the restaurant she took my hand. "Let's walk along the beach."

The beach was deserted except for two dogs copulating by a concrete bench which neither of us paid any mind to. No stars could be seen as they were washed out by the city lights but the sounds of the tiny waves rushing upon the sand was lovely.

"It's strange how people meet, isn't it Frank," Barbara told me more than asked. ''One day you're going through life in a set direction and then the next you're standing on a beach with somebody you really don't know but have a deep feeling for.''

"It is strange," I agreed.

"You know," she continued, "I was sitting in my house a few weeks ago bored and tired and lonely and I thought, well hell, I think I'll just hitchhike east, turn around and hitchhike back. And look, here we are." Barbara let go of my hand and scampered a few yards in front of me and turned. "You know? You have slept with me two nights and not even made a pass. You gay or something?"

"No," I answered seriously. "Just didn't seem right, was all."

"What is it then? You're not interested?"

"No, that's not it either."

"Well, what then?"

I looked out at the ocean and back at Barbara. "Don't want to be cheap, is all lady."

Barbara stepped back to me and took my hand once again. "Are we falling in love, Frank?"

I squeezed her hand. "I don't know. It's something." We walked back to her house in silence, each in our own thoughts.

While we were sitting in her living room, with her on the sofa and me in a chair, I thought back of all the years I had longed for love. There had been many girl friends. Each in their own way special to me but none of them ever making the bells ring, so to speak. Being in love had always been my strongest wish in life. I felt love would turn my life around and give me direction. Loving somebody would make me want to go out into the work force, make a living, buy insurance, do all the little American things that make up life. But when it came right down to it, I had never really fallen in love with a girl. When they left me, it was always for the same reason. I had no direction, I didn't want anything. I just shrugged it off and woke up the next day feeling the same way I had always felt when I was with them. But it was a different feeling I felt for Barbara. A feeling I had never experienced before. As she sat on the sofa I stood up and walked to her and touched her on the shoulder. "You make me feel good," I spoke. Then saying good night I went to my room and shut the door. As I lay on the mattress on the floor I heard her rise and go to her own room. Staring into the darkness of the room I knew I was afraid of the feeling that were budding inside of me. No job, no money, confusion over the war, jail. How could somebody like me be good for someone else? I fell asleep thinking about shared soap and towels and the curve of Barbara's lips when she smiled.

I awoke and it was still dark. Rising quietly I walked out and went into the kitchen and turned on the stove to warm up the coffee. I sat at the table illuminated by the street lamp outside and felt the warm content feeling a home can bring you, even though this was not my house. I never really had a house since I left my parents. Always moving, traveling. And now here I still was, wanting to travel up the coast and over the top of America, see the country one more time. Maybe this time I could find that key that would unlock my soul. But for the moment the darkened kitchen felt like a home. It was as though Barbara's heartbeat pulsed through the walls of the house, and in doing so made me feel a part of the house. I drank the lukewarm coffee and looked out the window. Cities are alien beings at night. Cloaked in fear they hide behind street lamps and stoplights that blink on and off for only the ones who must be out with the night. I could hear two cats fighting. I finished the coffee and went back to the room, stopping for a moment to look at Barbara's closed door. Back on the mattress I laid with eyes open and pulled deep inside of myself the feeling of the house.

I remembered lying on my cot in Nam. The night was hot and sticky. Occasional bursts of machine guns splitting the night. The roar of artillery. Lying and wondering what the people were doing back home, wondering how I really got there. Wondering, always wondering.

Barbara was standing over me with a green robe on, holding a tray. "Here you go, cowboy," she spoke. "Two eggs over easy with bacon and orange juice." I sat up and she set the tray on my lap and sat down on the bed. "Eat, eat. It will get cold." The eggs were perfect , the bacon crisp and not greasy, the juice fresh. When I was done eating she removed the tray and leaned over and kissed me fleetingly on the lips. "Now get up and get dressed. I want to show you around today. You can use the bathroom first."

An hour later we were standing out on the street. It was a beautiful day. Even the green sky was nice. "Where are we going?"

"To Disneyland."

"Disneyland it is then." To my surprise she opened the door to a Porche. "Sir," she grinned. I got in and she went around and got in the other side. "Old husband gave it me," she laughed. "Runs great."

"Nice car," I commented.

We flew through the traffic on the freeway but never made it to Disneyland. Somewhere along the way we stopped for lunch and ended up drinking wine and laughing the afternoon away. Driving back to her house warmed by the wine we listened to classical music on the radio and watched the world go by.

The evening as she was taking a shower I stood on the porch watching the sun go down and I knew I had to leave. Inside I felt as though I could stay forever with this beautiful blonde lady. Stay and go to computer school or bartender's school and work and come home and work and come home. On and on until I died. But in my heart I knew I had to go. There was the deep anxiety, almost fear. I had to know. There was something I had to find. Something out there pulled me. I turned and walked back inside the house, having made up my mind to tell Barbara about myself that night and be on my way the next morning. Or maybe that night if she booted me out.

Barbara came out of her room wearing a floor length shift dotted with white daisies. Her hair freshly washed and dried looked like captured sun rays. "Rather domestic, aren't we?" she cooed and her eyes danced. I smiled hiding the anguish in my heart. "I was going to take you to dinner but it looks as though you want to sit here in front of the television. That's what I want to do," she said.

I'll go to the store and buy something to cook for you," I volunteered.

She stepped over me and put her arms around my neck. Holding her I knew she had nothing on under the shift. She kissed me tenderly on the cheek and whispered, "Hurry back."

Walking to the store I knew I was a fool. Here I was with a beautiful lady, my heart bursting with feelings I had never felt before and I was going to leave. "Oh, Grandma," I lamented. "What am I doing?" But looking at the pea green sky, there was no answer.

At the grocery store there was a special on crab legs and I weighed out four pounds, got butter, four ears of corn and a bottle of white wine. A cheap bottle not knowing the difference between good and bad. I only knew you were supposed to drink white wine with fish. While standing in the checkout line, I decided to get another bottle of wine, just in case. Walking back to the house I felt happy, forgetting momentarily the task at hand. I felt a part of something but I soon lost the feeling when I knocked on the door and Barbara answered. "Just walk in, silly," she spoke.

I walked into the kitchen and set the sack down. "Look!" I played the part of the magician pulling the crab legs out of the sack. "Crab legs, corn on the cob and wine." Barbara took a large deep pan out from a lower cupboard. I took it from her. "You sit over there. I'll cook this." I led her to the kitchen table where she obediently sat down. Jesus, I thought to myself, if I was staying I could pick her up right now and take her to the bedroom, pull that shift up and nibble on her pert breasts. "You have a nice comfortable place here," I spoke breaking the crab legs.

"I like it," she answered.

After I had dropped the crab legs in the boiling water I husked the corn and opened a bottle of wine. Taking two wine glasses out of her cupboard I wiped them clean with a dish towel and set them on the table, filling hers first. I handed one to her, picked up mine and toasted, "May your dreams become your realities." Clinking them together we drank.

"My turn," she spoke, her lips wet from the wine. "May your heart always be warm." And we clinked glasses again. I walked over and dropped the corn into the pot of boiling crab legs. I found plates and silverware and set the table. After turning the heat off the pot I drained the corn and crab, put the corn in a bowl on the table and with a sharp knife split the crab legs. Then I melted butter and sat down.

"Well," Barbara commented. "Not bad for a cowboy." I reached for a crab leg but Barbara said, "Wait." She hurried from the table to her room and back. She put a candle on the table, lit it and turned off the other lights. Sitting in the candlelight with the smell of the crab and corn, peering into the angel glow of her face, I was like the melted butter in the bowl. You could have poured me on the floor.

We ate the crab and poured butter on the corn. We ate and laughed and refilled our wine glasses. There is something primitive about eating crab. Butter is sure to spill on your chin and fingers get greasy. Butter on Barbara's lips was the most erotic thing I had ever seen in my life. I don't know how but we ate all the corn, all the crab and drank a complete bottle of wine. "Did you buy another bottle?" Barbara half-burped, giggling.

With the wine of the afternoon and that bottle, I felt the resurgence of an old acid trip brewing in my mind. "Sure did," I answered. I opened the bottle and she picked up the candle and the two glasses and without a word I followed her to her bedroom. Her room was a frilly mass of motion. Weavings and photographs dotted the wall.

The bedspread was large and fluffy with lace around the edges and the window was covered with a lace curtain. I felt as though I was in the center of a flower.

"Take off your boots, cowboy."

I stumbled around removing my boots and sat down on the corner of the bed. Then I poured more wine. As I handed a glass to her I spoke. "To flowers." We drank deeply. She sat her glass down and moved over to me. I held my glass for protection. Protection to keep my hands from flying out and grabbing her breasts. She moved over to me on the bed and put my face between her hands and kissed me. Her tongue moved over my lips and I could taste butter and crab. My eyes closed and heaven waited. Moving back from me she took the glass from my hands and set it beside hers.

"Take your clothes off, Frank."

I stood and removed my clothes, embarrassed by my hard-on that stuck out like old glory. She wiggled out of her shift and lay back down on the bed with arms above her head. The candlelight danced on her form, making shadows between her breasts and thighs. I lay down beside her and buried my head in the nape of her neck, breathing deep the perfume and ocean of her. But then I sat up, my head bowed and spoke, trying not to look into her eyes. "I have to leave here, Barbara." Her hand touched my knee and her face seemed sad. But she did not speak. I wished she would call me names, holler, scream, do anything but just lie there and look sad. But she didn't. She moved her fingernails slowly over my knees, her breasts rising evenly with her breathing. Finally in a whisper she asked, "Why?" I started to reach for the wine glass but she stopped my hand. "No. Tell me why." I looked around the room. There were no walls to hide behind. "Go on, Frank. I'm a big girl. Tell me why."

I picked up her hand and kissed it. "Dear lady," I spoke. "Dear dear lady. I'm looking for something, Barbara. Something. I really don't know what it is but it's out there. Something along a highway or on a mountain, it's there. Something that will set me free. I'm a dead man. I guess all I believed in was this country as I grew up. Freedom, equality and justice." I stammered. "But I lost it. I lost it somewhere when I was nineteen walking through a jungle. I lost faith in man, I suppose. Back in the states I tried college. Tried to believe in the system again. Tried everything. Tried being a hippy, tried getting a job. Hell, I've worked as a truck driver, gas jockey, ranch hand, cowboy, dishwasher. You nane it. But it doesn't last long." I looked at the beautiful face on the pillow. "I just got out of prison, Barbara." She didn't move, she didn't shriek. Her eyes only softened. "I spent the last two years thinking about life and what I would do when I got out. And I decided I had to see this country. See this thing I fought for and believed in. See it and maybe whatever is missing in my body would appear. Besides a waitress in Texas, you're the only thing I can remember in my adult life that made me feel human."

"What were you in prison for, Frank?"

"Pot," I answered. I wanted to talk on, tell her my heart was breaking. Tell her it was only me. Tell her she was the most beautiful thing I had ever seen in my life and sitting on this bed with her was heaven. It was peace, it was starlit nights and rose sunrises, but I didn't.

Barbara sat up and put her arms around me. She kissed my neck and spoke softly. "Things happen for a reason, Frank. We go through life day to day, year to year, and everything happens for a reason. If I had not wanted to hitchhike we would have never met. If you didn't have to go find something we would have never met. But I know one thing. Frank. You make me feel warmer and fuller than anybody I have ever met in my life and I know I love you. And when you leave and go off to find what ever you have to find, I will be here. I'll be here." She lay back down. "Now, heart of hearts, you make love to me."

One can sleep with a lot of people. Fuck them, if you will. But there is a difference between fucking and making love. The body might not know but the soul knows. It was the first time in my life I had made love. We moved together like the wind and the tide. We touched each other with hope and desire and sadness. Afterwards we slept. A sleep of peace with no dreams, no tomorrows, no yearnings, no questions. I awoke still inside of her and we made love again. Slowly and I felt more love than I ever knew existed in me. When the sun shined through the window in the morning I gazed at her naked body blessed by the rays and I etched into my mind the look of peace and contentment on her face. When she awoke she smiled and reached over and touched my lips and a small tear rolled down her face.

"I love you, pretty lady," I murmured.

"I love you Frank," she answered.

I was sitting beside a tree along highway 101 now. The sun was setting over the ocean blocked from my view. She had driven me outside of town and let me out with my suitcase, said goodbye and turned the car and was gone. Not a wave, not a tear, not a good luck, not a smile. Just gone. Now she sits in the city. Maybe tonight she will go out dancing and some other man will hold her and feel what I feel for her. Maybe he will be a lawyer or a businessman with his feet solidly on the ground. But I know where she lives and I have her address and phone number and maybe one day I will be able to go back, knock on her door and she will smile at me and say. "I've been waiting, cowboy." And there still won't be any man's aftershave in her medicine cabinet.

CHAPTER III

The tree was not a home. It didn't have plants hanging in front of windows or a kitchen or a living room or bedrooms. It didn't have a bathroom with scented soaps and thick soft towels or a smile for me. It was just a tree. A tree beside the highway that countless cars passed everyday and probably didn't even notice it. But for the night it was my home. Leaning against its trunk I could see the stars and in the distance the glow from Los Angeles. The tree was comforting. It was alive. Some people say plants know pain and respond to different stimuli. Maybe because they take so long to grow they talk to themselves. But they talk so slow it takes years to complete a sentence. That is why we can't hear them. People are that way a lot. We get caught up in our lives and when we talk, we talk so fast nobody can really hear us. Maybe love is hearing somebody. Hearing them with more than with ears. With the heart or with tears.

I looked out upon the glow from the giant city. A city filled with rich people and poor people. People of every color. Mexicans streaming out of Mexico looking for hope. I thought about my old American history teacher telling us about the Spanish who first came to this country. Came looking for cities of gold and silver. I thought about the friars, the men so dedicated to a cause that they braved the land and the savages to bring word of a God. I wonder if they could sit here today if they would comprehend what they saw. Then I thought about all the people bombarded everyday with television and radios and jobs that left them tense and nervous and it seemed that man had not found his cities of gold and silver. But in not finding them he had created them. Every city from coast to coast was but a dream of gold and silver.

When I was young I did not know there were poor people. We were not rich but we were not poor either. We were comfortable and ate well. The first time I ever saw a big city I ended up in a slum by accident. I was appalled. This didn't happen in America. But there it was. I always thought what a waste of life. But now there are no answers, no cures for the ills. I discovered it's what you make of it. So you make it what you will and be glad you were not born in a slum.

There was a boy in the army. A boy like me at the time. I was white and filled with ideals of freedom and equality. He was black and bitter. We became friends out of some quirk. He was born in Harlem. Joined the army because they would feed him and ended up in the infantry fighting for equality for some people across the ocean while his own people were starving back home. We never talked about where we came from. We talked about pussy mostly. Good old army talk. When there is none around, what else do you talk about? He left the country three weeks before me. We said goodby behind the tent by the mortar ditch and I watched him walk to the truck for Saigon. He left me his address and I promised I would come see him. Watching him walk away is set frozen in my mind. There is nothing in the picture except his back. We shared a lot, walking through that jungle. Maybe too much. When I got out I went to see him. But it was strained from the beginning, when we met. He picked me up at the airport and and we rode in his Cadillac to his place. He was selling heroin and carried a gun. I still liked him. He lived on the top floor of an apartment building in a neighborhood that was always dark. In the other apartments in the building were whores. His. We sat in his room and drank a few beers but it was gone, what we had in the jungle. We were back in the real world. Back to being what we were. He was black and from Harlem and I was white, looking for the ideals I had lost during the war. He didn't need ideals. His world was black and white, as black and white as the heroin people were pumping into their arms and the men who screwed the whores. When he drove me back to the airport I felt empty. As we shook hands we could only shake our heads knowing times had changed. One redeeming quality of war. Everybody is equal. A bullet sets everything in its rightful order.

With my back against the tree I wondered where he was now. Maybe he was lucky and hadn't been caught and had a nice house somewhere and a wife who treated him well and some kids. But probably he was still in that apartment with his gun and heroin and his whores.

In the morning I walked to a truck stop not a mile from where I had slept. Inside the washroom I opened my suitcase to get out my toothbrush. There was small box inside. I opened the box and there was a bar of scented soap and a note. The note said simply, LOVE, BARBARA.

After cleaning up I went into the restaurant and had biscuits and gravy and coffee. Outside once again I stood by the door and asked truck drivers for rides as they came out. For an hour I heard the same line. "Sorry son, can't. Company won't let me. No insurance." Finally a man with short, stocky Popeye arms with tattoos and a cut off T-shirt came out. His hair was cut like a marine's and he wore black boots. The kind bikers wear. Looking at the ridges on his face caused by scowling, I decided not to ask him. As I was quickly turning away he grunted without stopping. "Going north? You can ride with me." I picked up my suitcase and followed him. He had a big Kenworth painted black and an enclosed trailer. "I own this mother fucker." he grunted crawling into the cab. "If I want to give people rides, I give them rides. Fucking company don't own me." He talked like an old marine, mean and out of the corner of his mouth. He had a sleeper on his rig and a wind diverter. Inside the seats were black leather matching the dash. All the knobs and various gauges were chrome. On the floor next to his feet was a sawed off double-barreled shotgun. "Don't worry," he spoke in a grunt. "It's just in case somebody wants to rip me off. I'm headed for Portland with a load of fur coats for Goldwaters. No smoking in my truck," he announced as we pulled out of the truck stop. "Smell up the cab." He turned on his CB, spat something unintelligible into it and we were off. He drove that rig like a master. We passed every car in sight. Eighty, eighty-five, ninety. He shifted and downshifted and cussed at fourwheelers and other drivers and ate up the highway. As he passed women drivers he always craned his neck to look at their legs or down their blouses. "Good view up here," he commented. "You can't believe some of the things I've seen from up here. A lot of highway head going on in this world." I was so fascinated watching him drive and glancing at the speedometer that I didn't watch the scenery.

Before I knew it was dark and he was pulling into a truck stop. "I'll fill this cocksucker up and we'll eat and hit the road again. Where are you going anyway?"

"I don't know," I answered.

"You wanted or something?" he scowled looking at the shotgun.

"No, I'm not wanted."

"No, suppose you're not. As thin as you are you couldn't get by in prison."

He ate a double cheeseburger and fries and drank more cups of coffee than I could count. I had a hot roast beef sandwich but the beef had to have been cardboard. "Food is shit here," the driver grunted. "But I like it here. They don't come up to you and smile and say hello. They just take your order, bring you the food, give you the check and leave you alone. I like that." I noticed the tattoos on his arms. One read: DON'T FUCK WITH ME, and the other, BORN TO DIE. I liked him. He was a loner and I've always been partial to loners. Done with eating, he picked up both checks. When I started to protest he held out his hand. "I'll get it. You get the next one." We walked to his rig over the grease slick concrete and by the hundreds of trucks idling, sitting in rows like primeval beasts ready to go forth into the unknown. Back in the truck he reached back into the sleeper and pulled out a large thermos bottle. Then he poked around in the glove box and took out a small tin. Opening the tin he popped two pills in his mouth. "Want one?" "Sure," I said. "Why not?"

Then we slurped down the coffee on top of the speed and he blasted onto the highway. As he got her into high gear I felt the speed coming on. The driver turned on his CB, pushed the mike and hollered. "This is American Dreamer. Comin' at you America!"

A woman's shrill voice answered his call. "Dreamer, you're going to be stopping tonight!"

"No, honey," he answered. "Going on to Portland. Catch you in a few weeks."

"I'll still be here," came the reply.

The driver laughed and looked over at me. He was eerie looking in the dash and overhead lights of the truck. "Women all over the country keeping us truck drivers laid. Maybe up in Portland I'll line you up with some. You just divorced or something, not knowing where you're going or anything?"

"No, just need to get out, is all."

"Ever been in a truck before?"

"No, drove some five tons and things working on ranches but never anything like this."

He laughed a deep genuine laugh and for the first time he didn't grunt when he spoke, "Last free thing in this country, son. Last free thing, this highway." He paused then said, "Between checks, that is."

The driver, not telling me his name or asking me mine, drove faster at night than during the day, once the speed got him. Armed with his CB and radar detector, he knew where all the police were and cruised by them at fifty-five miles an hour. Everytime he went by one he said the same thing. "Punk bastards. Murderers and thieves running all over the country and these cocksuckers are out there giving people tickets so judges and senators and governors and people like that can have big salaries." I had never thought about it before but it was true. Passing another truck doing about ninety, he spoke. "People who don't want to drive fast should have another road. A slow road. People who want to go fast would have a fast road. Even the fucking Europeans don't have speed limits."

The more I rode with the truck driver, the more I liked him. There was a simple freedom that flowed through his veins and through the engine and out the stacks of his truck. Every time I get a ticket now I wonder how many stores are getting robbed or how many people are getting killed while this police protector of mine is acting like some bad ass writing me out a ticket hiding behind his sunglasses.

"You know, I was a marine in the war," the driver hollered over the crackling CB and the sound of the engine. "Not in that pussy fucking' Vietnam war but the real war. Wasn't any year hitch then." He scratched his head. "Vietnam boys, even if they were short timers, they still got screwed. But that's how it is. Everybody gets screwed sometime. You get over it. Ever since the war this country has gone to shit. Fuckin' government has gone to shit. Hell, we got us actors and nothing but rich folks running the son of a bitch. What the fuck do actors and the rich know about the real world?" He laughed a deep laugh and sipped his coffee. "But let me tell ya' son, even with actors and fuckin' rich people, this country is still the best. Still the best," he repeated. "Let them communist fuckers come over here and try to take this country. You'd see how tough we were. We'd push their asses right back into the ocean." I listened to the steady stream of words that poured out of the driver's mouth. Taxes were high, cops were lousy, people were fucked, government was soft. But always, always, somewhere in the chatter, this country was the best. A little messed up but the best. "You know, one thing is you can always get back on your feet here. Always, you get out and show you got a little guts and you can get going. People will help you." I could see this driver wading through the jungles of Guadacanal, cursing and bitching about the fucking president and the shit-head rich people but firing his gun and throwing grenades and willing to die for the land and for his home.

It was silent for a few moments and I glanced at the speedometer. He was driving fifty-five and in the shadow of the dash lights it looked as if the wrinkles on his face had softened. "My father was a marine," he spoke softly. "I was raised by a marine. Taught that no matter what, your country was right. Everybody make mistakes, even countries. My father fought for the Europeans. I killed Japs. You know, I killed more Japs than I could ever count. Killed so many I reached the point where I was tired of killing them. I realized they were fighting for what they believed in, just like me. Funny, huh? I don't hate Japs. I even like Jap food. Father taught me that. Once you beat a man, you help him up. You dust him off, tell him it was a good fight and help him up. This country helps the world and you know, son? That's what's going to kill us. But at least we will go down for an ideal.'' The driver's voice was low now. Another man spoke. Not the tattooed gorilla but a thinking man, a man who had seen life. ''That's all you got in life, son. Ideals. Nothing else is real. You have to stand for what you believe. You have to, even if it gets you killed, 'cause if you don't, then you're a hypocrite. Being a hypocrite is worse than being a coward. I'm sixty-five years old now. Got me a wife and girl friends, my kids are grown. Old woman stayed by me for forty years. War, peace, drinking, whoring. She has always been there. I love her more than my life. There's something to say for that. For all these years, when I come home I just give her my paycheck. You gotta trust someone to give them your paycheck.'' And then he was silent and we drove into the night at fifty-five miles an hour. The cars passed below us and the sleeping houses with their porch lights on. The CB crackled but he did not answer. I think he offered me a ride because he wanted to talk to someone. Talk to someone and then be silent and not be alone with the night. Some nights people just don't want to be alone.

As I sat looking out into the night high above the rest of the world I realized this man was my father's age. And for the first time I understood each generation had its own problems. Its decisions to face, it complications. And you face them, one way or another you face them. Then I thought of the driver's wife, home somewhere, waiting. I wondered if Barbara could wait. If one night I could go out and get drunk and crawl back home with the dawn. If she would help me into bed and know it was nothing serious, I just had to get drunk that night. And I thought maybe love was just knowing men were merely men and women merely women. Nothing more and nothing less. And love was how hard you wanted to work at it. The speed was rushing through my mind as I sat vibrating from the highway and I thought of Barbara sleeping in her bed, surrounded by her room that was like the inside of a flower and I wanted to jump out of the truck and head back to LA but I didn't. Instead, I looked into the darkness of somewhere in northern California and thought about a woman who loved a man enough or was loyal enough to stay with him for forty years. I knew it wasn't because of the money or because the driver was handsome.

Just before dawn the driver pulled into a rest area. He yawned and crawled into the sleeper. "Stretch out on the seats and catch some sleep," he spoke as he tossed me a blanket through the curtain. "I'll wake you." Soon I heard his snores from the sleeper. I lay across the seats and before sleep came over me I thought about all the truck drivers in America blasting from coast to coast eating pills and think about the world. Somebody had to think about the world, nobody else seemed to.

About noon the driver shook me. Outside it was raining. We scampered to the restroom, washed and shaved and were blasting once again down the freeway. Large sprays of water curling back behind the tires made me feel we were a speed boat. The driver did not speak to me but rattled on and on to the other drivers on the CB. Most of the passing drivers he knew. They talked about baseball, weather, but mostly they talked about the president and politics. At exactly five PM we crossed into Oregon and a few miles down the road he pulled the truck into a long line of other trucks waiting to be weighed and taxed by the state. "Highway taxes," he told me. "They tax you by how much wear they feel your rig is doing on their highway. But then the federal government gives them the money for the highways anyways." He laughed a short sarcastic laugh, emphasizing the irony of it all. With the taxes paid, we were once again on the freeway with the lush green of Oregon passing us by. At around seven he pulled into a truck stop and I realized I had not eaten all day and I was starving. The speed was wearing off. "Good food here," he mumbled carrying his thermos bottle as we walked into the cafe.

The driver said hello to several other drivers before we sat down in a booth reserved for truckers. A pretty young girl, maybe sixteen, came to our table with two glasses of water and two cups of coffee on a tray. She smiled expansively and the driver smiled back. As she walked away I noticed she had a slight limp. She came back for our order and when she did, she handed the driver a note written on Red Chief writing paper. He ordered bacon and eggs and hot cakes and I ordered fish. He read the note while I ate my soup. I tried not to watch, learning in prison you don't invade a man's privacy, but I could not help but notice his eyes soften. He folded the note and put it in his billfold, glancing at me like he wanted to talk but just sipped his coffee instead. When the girl came back with our order he patted her hand tenderly and she smiled while doing a small pirouette for him. "Lovely," he whispered. Just then six or seven other truck drivers from around the cafe stood up and started applauding. The driver waved them off but I could see he was pleased.

He wolfed his food down and then got up saying. "Take your time, I'll be back." When he was gone the young waitress came to take his dishes away. "You know Bill?" she smiled.

"No."

"I love him," she answered. I smiled. "I can walk like most people now. Soon even the limp will be gone. Bill and a lot of drivers put in money for me to get my leg straightened out. My family couldn't afford it. Bill drove me to the hospital in Omaha in his truck for the operation and then they sent a plane ticket just a week ago for me to come home. I haven't seen him 'til now." She walked away with her slight limp. About twenty minutes later Bill came back in and walked over to the young waitress handing her a small bouquet of daisies. She set her tray down and hugged him around the neck. I looked at his arm with the BORN TO DIE tattoo on it as he patted the girl gently on the back. He waved at me and I got up with the check. I paid. It was my turn.

Outside it was still raining. "A lot of rain," I commented.

"Shit, it could rain in this fuckin' state for months. You live in this bastard long enough and moss will grow between your toes and your fingers will get webbed and your tongue long like a frog's. And all you'll think about is eating bugs." But then he laughed a deep jovial laugh. "But I love the rain. Something about it. It covers you like a blanket. You know what I mean? It washes out bitterness or something. Like a shroud. Hell, I can't explain it," he scowled. "But it's nice." As he climbed back into his truck he waved towards the restaurant and I saw the waitress standing by the window waving. "She sure is a sweet little thing," he mumbled to his steering wheel as he once again headed the beast towards the freeway.

I didn't know what time it was but it was dark when we rolled into Portland. He made a call and we drove through the city traffic to a Goldwaters where he backed the monster into an unloading dock. Men unloaded the furs. I saw a fortune go by my eyes. I overheard one of the foremen talking to the driver. "Somebody robbed a load of furs in New Mexico last week."

"No shit," Bill spoke, not sounding a bit afraid. Then he added, "Thought about it once or twice myself."

The foreman laughed. "Can you imagine, all that money in coats? More money in one of those coats than I make a year." They both whistled and shook their heads.

Once unloaded Bill called a depot and luckily before midnight he was loaded once again, this time with Japanese cookware wanted in Seattle. "Going to Seattle. Want to come along?"

"Sure," I answered without hesitation. "But maybe you should know my name. Frank, name is Frank."

"Name is Bill," he answered and for the first time we shook hands. He drove the truck to a truck stop and parked. He left the engine running as usual and took a deep breath. "First we'll go drink us a few beers and then we'll get in and drive a few hours and sleep somewhere down the road." He locked his truck and I walked beside him as we went through the drizzle down the way from the truck stop to a small white wooden tavern with a Miller sign in the window blinking off and on red. Inside were other drivers. It was not a place where you stopped in after work for a friendly martini and conversation about golf or the stock market. We sat in a corner booth by the juke box that was blaring country and western music. A short plump woman in a grey sack dress came over.

"What'll it be, Bill. Beer or pussy," she spoke matter of factly. In the dim light it looked like she needed a shave.
"Beer. Pitcher and two glasses." He reached into his pocket and took out a pill box. "Want one?"

I started to say no but decided what the hell as Bill popped one into his mouth.

"Live on these bastards on the road. Get used to them after a while. It's important you eat before taking them though or in time you haven't eaten in weeks. Stay on the road long enough and you have to ask people where you are. But you find out after a few years it really doesn't matter. People about the same wherever you go."

The speed was bitter but the cool beer was wonderful. I felt relaxed sitting and looking around the dimly lit bar filled with men that looked as though they would rip your head off any minute. It was funny but looking back on the last days in the truck I had not thought about all the normal garbage one thinks about. I didn't think about not having money or a car. Didn't worry because I didn't have a house or my taxes were due. Hadn't thought about the communists much except when Bill brought them or the bomb up. I wondered how I had made it through the last day without thinking about all those things. Before I knew it the pitcher was gone and we were slurping on another one. Bill seemed to be somewhere off in the ozone and I was doing just fine. On the second glass of beer from the second pitcher I suddenly had a pang of loneliness run through my chest. I thought of Barbara back in L.A. She was splashing in the ocean with her bikini on and another man was sitting on the towel watching her. I remembered the goose bumps on the top of her breasts and the way the sand stuck to her toes. Lord, it was wonderful to miss somebody. At the same time on the jukebox a Let's-Cry-In-Our-Beer song came on and the entire bar of truck-driving, speed-freak, red, white and blue beer drinkers all grew silent as they thought of some lost love in their life. When the song was over the bar returned to it normal level of loudness.

"Well, you ready, Frank?" Bill asked. His eyes were gleaming so I knew the speed was taking effect.

My foot was wiggling as I answered, "Let's get that black bitch on the road."

Bill put his arm around my shoulder as we walked out the door. I felt like a gorilla wanted to look closer at the side of my face. Back on the street he looked at me seriously. "I kind of like you. At first I thought you were a hippy or something, but I kind of like you." I felt touched and relieved but knew that to Bill anybody who didn't believe in the cut and dry was a hippy.

We didn't talk much during the drive to Seattle. I spent my time looking out the window and trying not to think about Barbara. I would see a particularily spectacular sight and wish Barbara was there to see it. I thought how she had not been alarmed about me being in prison or the war. I missed her tenderly.

In downtown Seattle, I climbed down from the rig for the last time, shook hands with Bill and walked away. It was a bright sunny day. Above the brick buildings sea gulls circled and I could smell the salt water. Standing on a pier I gazed once more out upon the ocean. It was not the water of California. Here the water was cold and deep blue. Here the fishing boats set out for Canada and

Alaska. Islands dotted the view, with tall pine and spruce trees
growning out of the moss-covered sides. I thought of Bill as I stood
on the pier. I could see him killing Japanese during the war and
then beating some poor American with his fist who didn't want to
help them. I could see him standing up and shouting at ten men
over what he believed, knowing damn well he was going to get his
ass kicked. And after getting it kicked, yelling at them again. I
could see him with his Born To Die and Don't Fuck With Me tattoos tenderly helping a girl who was born with a twisted leg into
his black truck and driving her to Omaha after he and his friends
had saved for her operation. As I stood looking out at the whitecaps
and with the cool swirl of the north Pacific Ocean breeze on my
face I loved the bastard. A man who had driven me almost the
length of the country without asking my name. Who bought me
dinner and let me sleep in his truck. I loved him. Maybe in some
strange way he loved me although he never knew that at one time I
was a hippy and I had fought in the pussy war, as he called it. I
would have liked to have had Jim the hippy and Bill and me sit in
some dark bar somewhere and throw a few down. Throw a few for
ideals and a country, although bad, was still our country and the
right to be what you wanted to be if you had the balls. That night I
ate steamed crab on the wharf and slept in a bus station wondering
where Bill was and if he had eaten his bennie and picked up some
other hitchhiker on the bum and down on his luck because he
needed somebody to talk to or because everybody deserved a break.

CHAPTER IV

I spent two days walking around the piers in Seattle, eating
crab and shrimp and more or less marveling at the ships. Being
raised mostly in the west I always thought about the ocean. Seattle, with its rock beaches and cold water and drift wood, was more
of what I considered to be ocean than California. It was wild and
free, cold, forboding, not made to surf on or for getting a tan. Made
for dressing in rubber suits and to bring back fish. I watched for

hours the scampering crabs that came out of the water invading the beaches to each whatever they could. I threw garbage to the seagulls and watched them dive and make faces at each other over it. I walked along the rock beaches and wished Barbara was there at times. But mostly I enjoyed the isolation I felt on the beach. I thought about ships coming into the harbor and loading up quantities of furs in the early days. It brought to life the terrible tales I had heard about the warlike Indians who used to live on the coast and left totem poles with firece faces rotting in the lush and dense cover of the rain forest. People's skins were white here, bleached out from the rain and lack of sun. But everything seemed clean from the water, although Seattle, like any other big city, was covered with its green air and clear pollutants.

That afternoon, after trying for and being denied a job unloading boats, I was wandering along the pier wondering what I would do to replenish my quickly dwindling fortune. I sat down on a wooden green painted bench to watch the seagulls. The day was overcast but pleasantly warm and I had some dried bread from a sandwich I had eaten the day before and had saved. If you can attract one gull with your offering, in time there will be other squawking and making fierce gestures at one another over the meager crumbs you throw them. I think the gulls do it just to entertain the bored humans that throw the bread. They always seem to have as much fun as the bread thrower. I was breaking up my bread when an old man walked up and sat at the other end of the bench. I smiled and he smiled and he reached into his pocket and pulled out a pack of Canadian cigarettes called Players and lit one. He had on a blue sailor's cap with gold trim, a clean white sweater, baggy jeans, and slip-on rubber soled shoes. His face was clean shaven except for a long white moustache that curled majestically at the ends. I finished breaking my bread and started looking at the sky. Presently a seagull with brown on the chest flew slowly by and I tossed the bread into the sky. With a quick dip of his wings he dove at the bread and grabbed it with his beak.

"Good one," the old man muttered. The seagull circled eyeing me and another offering shot into the sky. He captured it once again before it hit the ground. I laughed and the old man laughed. Off in the distance several gulls moved in and I threw one more piece of bread into the sky before the competition arrived. He caught it expertly, as if to say, "It's easy man." The old man laughed again. There were four seagulls in the area and each offering was met by the rustle of many wings and more reckless diving trying to outmaneuver the other birds. With each toss the old man and I laughed. When the bread was gone the gulls didn't hang around for very long. If there wasn't any bread there wasn't going to be a show and they flew off in their slow even-paced way. Gulls living around those piers were not hurting for food. As seagull life went, it was a pretty posh job if you were not picky about your diet.

The old man coughed and threw away the cigarette butt. "I like french bread," he commented. "You let it dry up real good and when you break it up most of the pieces have a bit of crust on them and they fly better than ones without crust."

"Never thought of that," I commented, "but it sounds logical. First rule of bread tossing is bread needs a bit of crust for better propulsion." I sat back on the bench wishing I had more bread. The old man pulled a piece of bread from a paper sack I had not noticed before. Judging from the curve of the crust it was French. We both eyed the horizon and sure enough within a few minutes there came a seagull in the sky. The old man, with little effort, sent the bread into the air and sure enough it flew three times as high as my white cut bread with little crust. The seagull, spying the offering, dipped a wing and captured it. In less than thirty seconds there were over twenty seagulls circling overhead. They had heard he was tossing French bread, not cut bread. He tossed and we laughed. He had a game of trying to get the bread to a certain bird with each toss and when he succeeded we both laughed with the success. It seemed he tossed bread for hours. All around us were piles of bird droppings unthankfully dropped in our vicinity. After several close calls the old man just smiled. "Perils of feeding the birds," and went on gleefully tossing. When the sack was empty he folded it up slowly and put it in his back pocket. Then he took out his pack of cigarettes and lit another one. He offered me one. "No, thanks. I quit," I told him. Which I had but I still craved them at times. We both sat, he smoking, both of us looking out at the ocean and the sky and the seagulls swirling and diving around a man and a woman a few hundred yards away.

"Looks like you fed gulls a long time," I spoke wanting to say something

"Fed them from here to the tip of Alaska and back for years. I like seagulls. They've been good to me and I've been good to them," he answered. "You can learn a lot from seagulls." I was wondering what you could learn from a seagull when he went on, "Watch them. They never seem to be in a hurry. They just fly around and look and sooner or later they find something to eat and they eat it. Teaches you. You don't have to be in a hurry in life and if you're not picky you always seem to get by. Just let it come to you. Just let it come. And little effort and it all works out."

I thought about that statement for a while not really knowing if I believed it or not but knowing I should have consideration for age and wisdom, I said nothing.

"Want to go drink a beer?" the old man asked.

"Sure," I answered.

He stood and led the way down the pier, to the right and down an alley that at night I don't think I would have entered. We went into a small bar definitely not meant for the tourist trade. Above the door in red paint was written The Dancing Seagull. Inside the bar it smelled of fish and the ocean. Decoration consisted of some fishing nets thrown in the corner and a few glass net floats hanging from nails in the wall. We sat at the bar and the bartender had to be the old man's brother.

"Philip, give me and the young man here a beer." The bartender didn't say anything. Relatives don't have to talk to relatives unless it's Christmas or Thanksgiving. After Philip brought the beer the old man added, "And an order of fish." Philip shuffled back in a moment with a piece of newspaper piled high with brown nuggets of deep fried fish.

"Two bucks," he spoke dryly. I paid the bill, the old man not even trying to reach for his wallet. I figured then he was a bum hitting me for a meal but I really didn't care. What the hell. In a few days of no work I would be a bum myself. The fish was delicious. The beer too warm. With the two beers gone and the fish eaten, I ordered more beer and more fish figuring maybe the old man was hungry. This time he paid. He wasn't a bum, I was.

"What are you doing in town besides feeding seagulls?" he asked looking from the bar down at my cowboy boots.

I wanted to tell him I was a graduate student working on my masters in ocean biology but I just looked at him and then felt stupid. "Looking for a job so I can get back on the road."

"Hmm," is all the old man said. In a moment he looked back

over at me and said proudly, "I'm 79 years old."

I didn't know what to say. It was another of those war and God statements. What can you say? I chewed on more fish and drank my beer, which that time was ice cold. I hate it when stockers don't move the cold beer to the front of the coolers. The whole world would be a better place if they did.

"You want more fish?" he asked. I shook my head. "Another beer?" I nodded my head. He paid again. "You want to hear my story?" he asked.

I sipped the beer. "I'd love to."

"Come on over here." I followed him to a small table by a dirty window and sat down. He looked at me closely. "You remind me of myself when I was your age. Don't worry, it ain't nothing. It all passes. Everything passes. Philip!" he hollered. "Keep them coming only don't tab them now. I own this place," he told me. "Sometimes I pay, sometimes I don't. I own twenty bars all over this town. This one I like. Wife is in Reno now. I hate Reno. Used to own fishing boats. Too old for fishing boats. Own bars now. Everybody drinks. I've got bars for rich people and poor people. Everybody drinks but I like this one. This one is real. This one is dirty and it smells of beer and cigarettes. It smells like the street. It smells like men, men who keep trying, trying to be something but never really quite making it. That's my brother behind the bar. He likes this one too." Philip walked over with two more beers. He still didn't speak. I pictured myself getting shanghaied and thrown on some freighter for China. The old man took a hearty swig of his beer, lit a smoke and looked out of the dirty window. "I'm Portuguese. Or maybe used to be I should say. My father was Portuguese and so was my mother. I'm American now. When I was a boy we lived in New York. My father unloaded fish boats until he died. When I was young I always dreamed of being something. I wanted to be a big businessman and have a fancy car." The old man smiled a fleeting reflective smile. "Not a bad dream. I was ashamed of my father when I was young. He didn't fit in with my dream of being a big shot. He didn't have good clothes, we didn't have a car and he always smelled like fish. He used to get drunk once a week, Saturday night when he did not have to go to the docks on Sunday. He and my mother would go out and she would bring him home drunk. It used to get me angry but it never bothered my mother. She loved him. I was seventeen years old

when my father was dying. Cancer all through his body. I went into his room alone because my mother told me he wanted to see
me. I remember standing there and for the first time I saw pride in
my father's eyes. Even torn up with pain and almost dead, his eyes
were dark and dancing. Gypsy eyes, my mother called his eyes
years later when we were talking after we had become friends. I
stood by my father's bed and I started to tell him I was sorry about
being ashamed of what he was. I don't know exactly what I said
but when I was done he waved at me his beaten hand connected to
the shriveled up arm and shook his head and told me I was only a
boy, what did I know. He motioned for me to pull a chair close to
the bed and sit down. He was very weak and could not talk loud.
While I was sitting he was talking to the ceiling more than to me. I
think it was his soul talking. He told me about his father back in
Portugal when he was a boy. He told me about going out on the
ocean. He told me about the loneliness and fear and danger. And I
knew then that my father had come to America for me, not for
himself. He had come to give me a chance." The old man paused.
"I didn't know my father until after he was dead but I suppose all
men are that way. It is one of the curses of being a man.

"After high school I came out here to Seattle. For four years I
worked doing anything I could do on the docks. I unloaded boats, I
did dishes. Unlike my father with a family, I only had myself and I
saved my money. I lived in the cheapest rooms I could find and ate
as little as I could. Then with my money and good luck I borrowed
enough to buy a fishing boat. I named it DAD and I knew my
father's soul was in the boat. He had his dream. He rode the ocean.
There is nothing like the ocean. It's not like anything else in the
universe. When your feet are on the land you know where you are.
Even flying you know what is below you. But on the ocean you are
always moving over a mystery. Down in the deep there are things
man will never see or know. The ocean is a secret place. I didn't
really love fishing. Fishing is a hard, cold job. It was only the
ocean. Later when I had three fishing boats, I always thought about
quitting, letting somebody else take my place. I would tell my
wife, I'll stop. I'll stay home and not go. At first she believed me.
But then after a few years and I had found an excuse to go at the
last minute, she would just shake her head and say if she couldn't
live with it, she shouldn't have married a fisherman.

"Some of the happiest moments of my life were spent on the

ocean and some of the loneliest. My first wife died when I was off the coast of Alaska. She died in her sleep with no pain. When I came home the house was cold and I looked at the little things she had done. The small doilies, pictures, afghans she had made. I still have those things in a box. Funny but out on the ocean I used to think about being alone but I never thought about her being alone. Alone in the house, sewing, needlework. But that is the life of a fisherman. It's part of the job. Every life has some drawbacks, some more than others.''

The old man took a swig of the beer and coughed and lit another cigarette. He looked at my beer and seeing it empty signaled to his brother who brought me another one.

''I think I did not feel for two or three years after my first wife died. I can't remember that period of time clearly. Oh, I can remember certain things I did. I remember the largest catch of salmon in one day in the history of my boats. I remember a storm up close to Kitamat that I thought we were for sure sucked in. But that's about it. I remember not sleeping at night, crying and drinking but I can't remember the feeling of it all now, just the thought. I learned that I too was going to die and I had never thought of that before. I also learned that life goes on. That's the hard part, I suppose. Life goes on. If we could just lay down and die when it gets tough, it would be a lot easier.'' He ground his cigarette out and exhaled the last puff. It was growing dark outside. He smiled at me the way my father used to when for some reason he felt close to me or had some momentary flash of insight that what happened to me wasn't his fault. ''I'm tired son. If you're around tomorrow we'll talk more.'' I finished the beer and stood. As I started to walk off he pointed his finger at me. ''Just remember. French bread and break it so each piece has a bit of crust on it and if you need a job, show up here in the morning and my brother will let you in. You can help him clean up.''

Walking down the alley toward the pier I passed many men in the shadows. Men with rubber boots on, walking quickly towards the bar and the beer. The bar that was real.

That night I slept on a bench close to the ocean. I didn't really sleep but I was rested when the sun rose and the squawk of the seagulls began to roll over the wakening day. It was a pretty sight. The piers empty but bathed in gold. Within the few minutes of the sun coming up the many fishing boats began to come in and at the various fish markets the nets and boxes were dumped. I thought of the old man going out on the face of the sea and the smell of fish and the danger and I knew it was not for me. The ocean for me was more to look at, more for sitting and thinking about life than to live upon. She was too deep and mysterious and I was not Jesus and couldn't walk upon the water.

After a small breakfast at a cafe for working men, I walked to the Dancing Seagull. After knocking on the door for several minutes and getting no answer I left. It was just as well. I walked to the bus station and bought a ticket for Bozeman, Montana. Why Bozeman, I don't know. Sitting on the bus I watched Seattle pass by. Another city bustling and spitting poison into the air. A city filled with young men and old men and thousands of stories. I was glad to be going and would never see the old fisherman again. It is nice to know only half the story and still be able to picture him as a young man out on the ocean. By dark the bus was rolling through the plains of eastern Washington. I thought about Barbara and the night we lay together under the stars as strangers. Love must be one large entity that circles the earth. Little particles of it break off at times and fall to earth landing on two people. I had never missed a girl the way I missed her. I knew I could make it through life and never see her again but there was a part of me that did not want this. Thoughts of kissing her again were like tiny pins piercing my heart.

CHAPTER V

A bus at night is like a church. During the day you can sit in a church and spend your time looking at the paintings or the way sun shines through the stained glass. But at night everything is covered with shadows and you peek momentarily at your soul not distracted by what is around you. If you are lucky and there is a God, you can visit Him for a few moments. A bus at night is this way. You can't see the grime or the cigarette butts ground out on the floor. You don't see the rips on the seats. You only see shadows and in the distance the faint glow of the dash light shining like small benediction candles. I sat feeling peaceful, knowing it was only a momentary feeling. That soon, no matter what I did, the feeling would go and I would once again be filled with anxiety and fear. But for the moment I was peaceful. I wondered where the truck driver was at that moment. Blasting down some highway rapping on his radio. And I wondered if the old sailor lay in his bed thinking about his first wife that died and left him unfeeling for so long. I wish I could have told him I knew the feeling. The feeling of an unthankful war or prison but I am too young to tell people I might understand. Age in itself is not knowledge. It's just age. "Old age is hell," my grandmother used to tell me. And I knew she told me the truth. No reason to lie. What for? I looked out into the darkness and the occasional light that marked a farm house and wondered what life was going on in the house and if a person in the house could see the bus passing down the highway in the distance. And if there were such a person, were they like me, searching? If I met them could I say I saw you once through the darkness looking at me as I sped by on a bus and we would smile and be friends without really knowing each other. Like Barbara. Funny, it seemed Barbara was always in the back of my mind. Not a force that compelled me but a feeling, a longing that was sweet and bitter at the same time. It was like having a smile with you but you could not touch it and maybe it would have been just as good if it had gone away.

The bus stopped but I did not feel like going inside the neon world of the small bus station. Inside I could see a waitress move slowly and give the driver a cup of coffee but they did not speak. Even lovers do not speak this hour of the night. My mind wandered.

My grandmother was born and raised in a small farming community in Iowa. It was always a place I loved to go to when I was young. The land was nothing but corn, miles of corn. At night there were fireflies and I used to believe they were tiny Tinkerbells. When my grandmother married they moved into town and she ran a cafe and he was a janitor at the bank. I don't know if I could be a janitor but they were both proud and people genuinely liked them. It was a small town of less than three thousand people. There was a crazy man who lived in town. He lived in a small trailer on a few acres and grew corn and picked up people's garbage. He drove an old red tractor around town. Nobody seemed to mind. He never ran over a kid or a dog or cat and he always picked up the garbage on time and didn't make a mess. Everybody my grandmother knew bought his sweet corn. I can still see that crazy man riding through town on his tractor. He wore bib overalls and had a grey floppy hat and his chin was always cocked up into the air and his eyes seemed to only see the sky. He never talked but he always knew what people were saying to him. When I was a kid some of us boys used to go over to his house at night and throw rocks at his roof. I've killed people since than but looking back it bothers me more to have thrown rocks at a crazy man's roof. He never came out of the house. Maybe he was always asleep and didn't even know we were out there. It doesn't really matter. What matters is we did it. When I was older, 14 or 15 and in love for the first time, I was sitting on the porch with my grandmother looking at a squirrel run up a tree. The crazy man, now seeming very old, drove around the corner on his tractor. Being that I was older and in love, it suddenly dawned on me that this man had never been in love nor would ever find somebody to love him and I felt very sad for him. I looked at my grandmother and said, "He'll never be in love, Grandma." My grandmother looked at me for a moment and then spoke. "God loves him." A few years later I received a letter from my grandmother. I don't remember where I was but the letter read quite simply. "The garbage man was married the other day. He met a lady from Chariton who is simple but is as nice as she can be." I was happy. I thought about that a lot during my life. I could see them walking down the street with his chin stuck up in the air and his eyes looking off into the sky and with her wearing a plain cotton dress. It had to be a nice love. A tender love, a wordless love. Two simple people, not able to understand the complexities of life, not knowing there were presidents and dictators, taxes, not understanding God or the devil, just living and knowing enough to feel a bond with another human being.

A few years ago they died together. There was gas leak and they died during the winter in bed. I was in Vietnam and my grandmother wrote to tell me. The letter took me back from the war to the little town where crazy people could still live and a man was proud to be a garbage man. At the time it made the war make sense.

The bus lurched. I did not notice the driver leave the diner nor hear the door closing. As we pulled away I wished I had gone inside for a piece of pie or something.

I lit a match and looked at my watch. It was three AM, Barbara was probably curled in her bed, I hoped alone. I left her and wished she was not with anybody. Which didn't seem right. I could smell the ocean smell of her and see the way her eyes fluttered when she slept. It was like tiny elves were playing behind her eyelids. I wished I was there with her then. Now once again halfway in between somewhere. I felt the peace leaving my body and the tiny pangs of anxiety enter. It was like having too many cups of coffee and knowing it but drinking more. God, somewhere in the world with growing old and disease and wars and prisons there was something that was solid. Something one didn't fear but felt secure in. I knew it was not insurance. Simple people maybe were the truly blessed.

"Wake up, son. Wake up," the bus driver's voice rang in my ears as I moved shaking the cobwebs from my mind. "It's Bozeman, you get off here."

I struggled to my feet and zigzagged down the aisle of the bus like a drunk. Outside the bus the stench of countless buses idling filled my lungs. Small lines of people stood in front of buses like martyrs going into the mouths of lions. I felt as if I had lost hours out of my life. I didn't remember falling asleep. I just went off into the darkness, the lifeless, the dreamless. It was scary. I went to the bathroom and ran cold water on my face and brushed my teeth and combed my hair. A cowboy pissed and payed no attention to me as he finished and left without washing his hands. My face in the mirror was still me, much to my surprise. It seemed I went to sleep as me and woke up somebody else. I lost something inside that bus that I will never regain. "Dear Barbara," I moaned smelling the odor of piss and bathroom bowl cleanser around me as I tried to feel human. "Dear dear pretty lady. How is the soap in your bathroom and the thick soft towels that have caressed your body? And the neat little rows of perfume?" I was a complete idiot, there in the bathroom in the bus station in Bozeman, Montana, when I could have been in LA breathing green air but waking to the touch of a pretty lady with sun shining through the window, not standing in a bathroom in Bozeman, Montana, smelling piss.

I shrugged my shoulders, took a deep breath and went out into the terminal. I felt better sitting in the restaurant. Two cups of coffee and bacon and eggs and I felt halfway alive. I looked through the window and noticed that the people who passed by all had on cowboy boots. It was the west. The sun was up, it was summer time, I needed a job, and missed Barbara. Shit. What else could you say but shit?

If you have never been in a strange town needing a job and wondering what the hell you are going to do, then you haven't lived. When you have been in prison you always feel there can never be a time in your life that can be more down but when once again and you're back on the streets, you find that this statement is not always true. I walked down the streets of Bozeman towards the employment office. I could picture years earlier the cowboys riding down the street on horses, not in shiny Ford pickups with rifles in the back window and little holders for their hats on the inside of the cab. I could see bars with whores waving at the miners from the doorway and a sheriff who realized it was smart medicine to look the other way.

As I stood in line at the employment office I wondered if I looked as bad as the others in line. And if I did look that bad then maybe a life of crime really wasn't as bad as people made it out to be. The line moved slowly. When I finally reached the bored woman chewing gum she handed me a sheet of paper and told me to fill it out. I filled it out, lied a lot and stood in another line to hand it to another lady who reminded me of my high school English teacher who was going to look at my paper but knew without looking that I flunked it. When I handed it to her she gave me a number. "When you are called, follow the person who called your number," I was instructed. I looked around the office. There were a dozen or so people behind desks looking like they were bored talking to people needing work. If I had not needed the money so bad I would have walked out of there. I sat down in a row of chairs with the other jobless and waited. Within an hour an attractive lady called my name. She was friendly when I walked towards her and I felt better watching the way her dress swished as I followed her to her desk. She sat down and smiled at me, the type of smile that comes from working in a sad place for too long. It's a "I know, I only work here but really don't know if I can help you" smile. Employment through an employment office is only a temporary thing. A brief look at a better life. I returned her smile.

"Let's see, Frank," she began. "You say you were in the army, an infantry man. Learn anything in the army?"

I half-smirked. "Not much that does me any good out here unless you can get me in touch with the mob to be a hit man."

The lady smiled faintly. I could tell I had blown it and she would no longer be my friend. "Well, what have you done since you have been out of the army?"

"Odd jobs," I lied. I couldn't tell her I was a hippy trying to find myself and then spent time in jail for trying to find myself. So odd jobs will do. "I can drive farm trucks," I threw in, trying to get back in her good graces. "And I'm a good worker." She chewed on her pencil. I was feeling desperate. "Listen," I told her. "I don't want to get welfare or anything. I just need some work so I can get back on the road."

She looked at me and smiled a school teacher smile. "Come back tomorrow, Frank. I think I can get you a job."

"What do I do?" I asked.

"Just come in and ask for me. Miss Simpson. Okay?"

I stood, feeling humble for a moment and walked away as she called another number. She seemed honest. Maybe there was hope for work.

Back on the street there really wasn't much to do. I ambled along with one hand in my pocket carrying the suitcase halfheartedly. I had two hundred and twenty dollars and change to my name. If I had been a real criminal I would have just ripped somebody off, I suppose. But judging from the people I had seen in Bozeman, they would have just laughed and strung me up the nearest tree and left me for the crows to pick my bones clean. I walked for several blocks and came to a cheap hotel. It was a two story brick and the front concrete steps covered with dried chewing tobacco. I could see old men sitting in the lobby. Two were playing checkers and one was reading a paper. Inside it smelled of old tobacco and dust. It felt like an Egyptian tomb. The old men did not look up. A man walked out from a back room behind the counter and smiled slightly. He looked as though he had been sleeping. "Need a room?" he ask politely. I nodded my head feeling weary. "Eight bucks a night, bath at the end of the hall. Clean the tub when you're done." I gave him the money and took the key. The three men didn't seem to know I walked by them.

The room was small. A bed and a small end table with a yellowed doily on the top. A lamp was attached over the bed. There was a window that gave a view of the next building. I opened my suitcase and discovered to my delight that I had one set of clean clothes and I remembered the scented soap. I felt better. I had something to do. I would take a bath and put on my clean clothes and then do my laundry. The American work ethic had come through again.

The tub was the old fashioned type with legs. It was deep and the water could be adjusted with two handles, not like the modern fixtures. I soaked in the tub and smelled Barbara's soap and wished I had Barbara's towels and not such thin ones. I thought about being little when my brother and I used to take baths together. I always got him in the eye with the old frog in the water trick. My brother was not very smart then but now he's a school teacher and is married and has kids. He owns a house and a boat and a car and has insurance. Dumb kids don't necessarily turn out to be dumb adults. I stayed in the bath looking at the edge of the commode until someone beat on the door, mumbled something and walked off, obviously wanting to take a bath.

I asked the man at the desk where the laundromat was, he pointed more with his nose than with his hand. "Down to the corner, turn left and you can't miss it."

Laundromats are depressing places. There is always a sign on some machines stating they are broken. Broken from doing too many loads of wash by too many broken and beaten people. The people in laundromats are like the machines. Weary. Kids ran around, mothers stand there chewing gum and wishing they were rich and had a machine and dryer at home or better yet enough money to have somebody else do the wash for them. The soap dispensers look like slot machines that will never pay you one truly clean wash and the magazines are torn and twisted with articles cut out. I loaded the machine, everything in one load, put my money in and waited until the cycle started before going outside to stand by the door and watch the day like an old man. As I stood I noticed for the first time the mountains outside of town. The peaks were still covered with snow and I realized the air wasn't green. I started to feel better. Bathed, shaved, clean clothes. Life wasn't that bad and I could possibly get a job the next morning. A few people passed by but said nothing. Not many people speak to people standing in front of a laundromat even if they are clean. I went back inside and put the clothes in the dryer. Once again outside I thought about Barbara. I wondered if I called her would she drive up there in her ex-husband's Porsche and pick me up. I wondered if women ever thought about going out and fucking someone. I hoped they didn't. Men say, "Well, I think I'll go get fucked," or "I fucked her," or "Boy, would I like to fuck her." When you're young and still haven't slept with anybody, you can't wait. But when the day comes and you fuck somebody, you wonder what all the fuss was about. When you finally love somebody and make love, you know the difference. I always thought since the army that whores have to be the most lonely people around. They are always geting fucked but not made love to. Maybe not all of them though. I've seen some draped in furs and jewelry and they didn't seem to mind it. I still try to hold onto the belief that money doesn't buy everything but sometimes I wonder if it's true.

I walked back to my room, my clothes folded under my arms, feeling human again. It was nice. I thought about the fat lady back in Texas who gave me the pie and didn't have me pay the check. It had started with her, feeling human. I wondered if she had a washer and dryer.

With the clothes back in the suitcase I lay down on the bed. It felt good after sleeping on the bus. I thought back to all the nights in jail lying on my bunk thinking about this country. Trying to put a definition on everything. Honor, hope, valor, guts, pride. It seemed I had left the pen a long time ago. It seemed like it really didn't happen but it did. Somewhere in the past it had happened. Like when you're a boy and suddenly you're a man and you can't remember what it was exactly that made you a man. Everybody always tells you when you're a boy you should straighten up and be a man. A man. Some mystical thing every boy wants to be and boom, you're a man. It's a joke on you when you discover you're a man. Every man wants to be a boy again except a marine.

I rested on the bed but did not sleep. I spent the time wondering how many down and out people had stayed in that room, since people who are not down and out stayed at the Holiday Inn or the Ramada. I don't know what it is but old things always seem to connotate misery. People see a new building and they say, "Isn't it grand." But an old building is a poor old thing. It's like people. A new person is poked and coddled. An old person is a poor old thing. Maybe old things are glad to be old. If everything is miserable when it gets old, it must have been miserable getting old.

When it was dark I turned on the lights and walked down the hall to look in the mirror. The bathroom still smelled like the scented soap Barbara gave me. I didn't know what scent it was, but it was nice. As I went down the stairs I heard television behind closed doors and imagined they were in the rooms of the old men playing checkers. An old hotel for old men. I wondered where their children were. Probably in Phoenix or LA Not in Bozeman. Not enough industry in Bozeman. Not enough money to keep them. You can breathe the air so it must be poor.

Out on the street the neon world had lit up. A few bar signs blinked between the closed auto parts and department stores. Bozeman was not LA I walked down the street and went into the closest bar. I don't know why it is that people head for bars when there is nothing to do. I wondered what the cave men did with no bars. Headed for an empty cave? A bar is like a cave. Cool and dark, dangerous if you want it.

Inside an old wooden bar stretched the length of one wall. A mirror ran half of the length, reflecting the back of liquor bottles and leaving the impression there was twice as many bottles as there really were. The rest of the bar was filled with pool tables. "25 cents a game" hung from a card from a slowly revolving ceiling fan. There were fifteen or twenty cowboys in the bar. They looked up menacingly as cowboys do, some chalking their pool sticks and others nursing their beer. It was early. These were the single cowboys of Bozeman. I was not bothered by the stares. The cowboys sensed this and returned to whatever was important before I entered. It is an instinct in all animals to sense fear or not. After a war and prison I was not afraid of physical pain. I sat at the bar between two cowboys, nodded hello and ordered a Coors. Both men were beginning to feel the effects of drinking. One had his head down looking like he had just lost his love. The other one looked at me and spoke. "Bob. Name's Bob. New in town?"

I nodded my head. "Just passing through. Trying to pick up a few bucks and get back on the road."

Bob swigged his beer. "Yep, Hard times now. Hard times."

I swigged my beer and agreed. "Sure are. Hope it gets better."

Bob laughed. "Don't really matter if it does or not. Going to die anyway." Then he looked past me to the forlorn cowboy. "Cheer up George. Come on. She'll take you back."

George shook his head from side to side. "No she won't."

Bob laughed again, "People love misery," he told me with a wink.

I drank my beer. "Part of being a cowboy. Things are always tough and you're always stewing over some woman. Yours, his, or your mother."

"Where do ya' come from?" Bob asked.

I didn't want to say LA so I thought for a minute and muttered. "Kansas." Bob laughed. He laughed at everything. But it was contagious and I began to feel happy. I wanted to tell George it would be okay. Everybody loses a girl somewhere but bars are full of cheap advice. If he went to a shrink and paid sixty dollars an hour for the same advice, then he might listen.

"What did you do in Kansas?"

"Drove tractor."

"Beats riding a goddamned horse."

With my beer finished I ordered another one and one for Bob for making me feel good. I didn't order one for George. He could decide to take his remorse out on the world and bean me with a bottle. Lost love can be that way, very irrational.

Bob nodded his head thanks for the beer. "Ain't much work around here. Times are tough. Shit, most of the cowboys are guiding fishing trips now. And hunts. Not much cowboying left."

"What do you do," I asked.

Bob laughed again. "I'm lucky. I own a ranch. Keeps me busy and in hock with the government."

"Times are tough." I replied.

He twirled the beer bottle and mused. "Wouldn't know what the hell to do if times weren't tough. Would you?"

I thought about it for a minute looking at the rows of bottles by the mirror and felt like I had just been told a great truth in life. "Nope, guess I wouldn't." We both laughed and raised our beer bottles and drank together.

"Tough times," he said.

"Tough times," I echoed and we drained them.

The street was almost empty. A police car cruised slowly by but paid no attention to me. I looked left and right for a cafe and decided to walk away from the hotel to look.

My father's parents were farmers. His mother and stepfather

were farmers. Even then people divorced. Too bad when you realized even your relatives made mistakes. They worked hard. Iowa farmers. Cows, chickens, pigs, turkeys, geese, sweet corn, tomatoes and pickles. I would visit and watch my grandparents work and it was great fun to me. Fun to carry a token bucket of corn for the chickens or slop to the pigs. They worked all day and when it was dark they ate and went to bed and the next day they did it all over again. When they did take a day off the women worked in the kitchen cooking chickens and making salads and pies and then they all sat around and ate and talked about the weather. I never realized until I was older that they were poor and their lives were tough. They never seemed poor. They laughed and cussed and worked and ate and they never talked about being poor or how tough it was. I think my relatives made moonshine when they had to. The way people grow pot now. They needed the money and doing something for yourself was better than borrowing money. If my grandfather was alive now you could show him a credit card and he would just laugh. Money was what you kept in the cupboard in a cookie jar. If they were alive now and the farm had not been sold I could have gone to be a farmer. Never think about life or lost ideals or any of that. Just immerse myself in cows and pigs and the smell of dirt. And eat three big meals a day and tell everyone how the weather was changing every year. I could say that until I die. Then they would bury me in some rural cemetery where nobody would ever see my grave until little children one day would look at the stone and say, "Mommy, look how old this one is." But there are no farms like this now. The government has them now, tucked neatly in its pocket. It always wanted them. Farmers hate the government now. They sit around little towns on park benches and talk about the government getting the farms. And they've lost their hearts.

My grandmother talked about the farm. The snow, the mud, the corn ruined. The tornadoes, the drought. It was just part of being a farmer. What did a farmer know about commodities and land tax and borrowing. The government didn't tell them and it took the land.

The cafe was clean and plain. Wooden tables were lined neatly in a row with four chairs at each table. The waitress was young and pretty. Probably in high school. I sat at a table and took the menu from between the ketchup and sugar shaker. The menu was typed with the prices scratched out and raised higher. The waitress brought me a glass of water and smiled showing her braces. Then I knew why the prices had been raised.

"Roast beef sandwich," I spoke, feeling the beer.

She shook her head. "Beef is no good today. Have a hamburger."

"Okay. With everything on it. And a coffee and a large coke."

"Only one size coke. It comes in a can." She walked off and I couldn't help but admire the young legs. Some young man was going to smile and maybe end up in a bar like George.

The hamburger was delicious. No need for a waitress to lie I supposed. Back on the street I walked towards the hotel. It was cool outside, refreshing. I walked slowly and looked at the strange town. Everything was slower. No hustle, no bustle. A mountain town trying to stay a cowboy town. I hoped they wouldn't open a ski resort.

Back in my room I undressed and got under the covers. The sheets were stiff and the pillow hard but it was still comfortable. As sleep was about to overcome me, I thought about the cowboy sitting in the bar drinking beer and trying to cheer his friend up. "Things are tough." The old cowboy knew. Things have always been tough. Just like any other things in life. I supposed. You have to laugh or it will break you.

Miss Simpson at the employment center was breathtaking. Her auburn hair fell in smooth folds to the top of her shoulders and her eyes seemed alive, not covering a sadness like the last time I sat at her desk.

As I sat down I spoke, "You fell in love last night."

She looked amazed and then held out her ring for me to see the small diamond engagement ring. I nodded my head slightly and let her glow immerse me. She took a deep breath and ruffled some paper. "I have a job for you, Frank." It was my turn to feel amazed. "You said you drove a tractor in Kansas. Well, there's a ranch outside of town who need a tractor worker." She leaned over me like we were going to discuss a crime. "This job isn't through the agency. I know the man." She took her pencil and drew a map. "Follow this map and it will take you to his place. His name is Bob. Tell him you're the fellow Miss Simpson called about."

I took that map and stood. "Thank you. Thanks a lot." I turn-ed and walked away but then turned back to her. "Good luck with your marriage." She smiled. As I walked out I tried not to look at the other people waiting to be called. Outside I prayed I would not grow old without ever making it in some way. To be old and poor was not where to be.

After the war I used to visit a friend of mine in the VA hospital. The first time I went there I walked through brown corridors with the floors so polished you could see your face and I was appalled by the old men sitting in wheelchairs staring off into nothing. Living somewhere in the past because the present was unbearable. My friend was in a room with what remained of his right foot sewn to his left thigh. He had stepped on a mine and it took most of his foot and his right arm. There was a triangle bar above his bed so he could pull himself up into a sitting position with his left hand. The doctors had sewed his foot to his thigh so the flesh would grow back on it. They left him that way for over a year and then severed the flesh and he had a form of a foot. He got a check every month from the government. I took him magazines and books and little worthless things. We would sit and talk about the war. I think I grew more bitter because of him, not me.

They used to dress up the old men sitting in the hall on Veteran's Day, put on their old army hats and medals and take them downtown and set them down to watch the parade floats and the people passing by looking at them and feeling proud and sad at the same time. I have not seen my friend in years. When he was released he disappeared somewhere and never told me where he was going. I could imagine him hobbling down to get his check but I cannot picture him sitting beside the road with his medals as an old man watching the Veteran's Day parade roll by.

I walked back to my room and packed my suitcase. Nobody was in the lobby when I left. Following the map, I walked to the edge of town and stood holding out my thumb. The ranch I was go-ing to was called the Broken Drum and was about four miles out-side of town. The headquarters was another mile off the paved road. It was a beautiful day. Cars went by with fishing poles stick-ing out of the windows. The Madison and the Smoke flowed close to there. Famous trout rivers. I was glad I had jeans and cowboy boots but wished I had a fishing pole and enough money to go fishing for a month.

An old dented and rusted Ford pulled over for me. Inside was a woman in jeans and boots and a red wool western shirt. Her arms were as big as my legs and her shoulders made the shirt bulge. Her face and hands were tan from the sun and wind. "Need a ride?" she bellowed.

In the back of the truck were several rotten bales of hay and beer cans. I put my suitcase in the back and got in the truck. When I slammed the door, dust billowed up into the air and then slowly settled back down to its original location.

"Name's Kate!" she bellowed again over the noisy exhaust. I noticed the outline of a pack of cigarettes in her pocket over a large breast. "Where you headed?"

"Lady found me a job out here at the Broken Drum. Driving tractor."

Kate laughed. "Bob's place. Good man but he'll work your ass off."

I laughed. "I hope not. I need my ass. I sit down so much I wouldn't have anything to sit on."

Kate snorted and then looked out the window. "Gorgeous day, isn't it."

"Lovely," I answered. "The blue Montana sky seems to go forever."

"Poor man's wealth," Kate mused.

After a few minutes I asked. "How's the fishing around here?"

Kates face lit up. "Right now it's a little slow. The last of the runoff is coming down but in a few weeks it will be great. You like to fish?"

"Love it, but I haven't been in a long time."

"Well, when you get a day off, if you ever get one working for Bob, you ask him how to get to my place and I'll take you fishing."

"You got a deal," I answered.

Kate slammed on the brakes jarring me from my daydream and the old truck shuddered to a stop. "Go down that dirt road there and you'll see Bob's house. Good luck, boy." I got out and started to say thank you after getting my suitcase but she was off before I could speak. It was nice walking down the dirt road. On either side of the road were well-kept fields of just sprouting winter wheat. The fence was well maintained. Through one field a stream flowed, six to eight feet at its widest point but I knew it was full of trout. The kind you pop in a skillet of hot bacon grease and they're done in a minute. A few quarter horses lazed by a cottonwood tree and redwinged black birds darted around the last year's cattails in a marshy area beside the road. In the distance I could see the outline of cattle. As I rounded the bend in the road I could see the ranch headquarters. There was a white sign over the entryway with black letters proclaiming: BROKEN DRUM. The ranch house was a rambling log cabin with a grey shingled roof and not far from the house was a small cabin with a matching roof. There was a metal barn and two large hay sheds that were nearly empty from feeding cattle all winter. Several tractors were neatly parked by the barn and the farm equipment was all in line. "Man must have been in the army," I thought to myself. The house had tulips blooming in small patches and I could see a freshly worked garden. Beside the house, clothes were hanging limp on the clothesline in the windless day. Everything was neat and orderly. It smelled of care and pride. I walked down the entryway and four dogs ran up the drive way barking at me. One large dog that looked like a cross between a German shepherd and the devil ran at me with his fur standing straight up. Dogs have never bothered me. I always figured if you didn't show fear then they wouldn't bite you. But as this one drew nearer I became fearful. As the dog was about to lunge at me and I started to swing my suitcase, I heard a sharp command. "No, shithead!" The dog immediately spun in the air, landed on his feet wagging his tail and trotted towards the voice. The other dogs ran around me poking me with their noses, wanting to be patted. My heart was pounding and it was a pleasure to be alive and able to pat a friendly dog. I went up to the man standing in the front of the house and held out my hand. It was Bob from the bar. He laughed and we shook hands.

"Miss Simpson sent you out?" I nodded my head. "Hell, last night when you said you needed a job, I was about to tell you I needed help. But Miss Simpson had called me during the day saying she was sending a man out. Small world, isn't it? Follow me."

He turned and we walked towards the small cabin I had seen from the road. Inside there was a gas stove against one wall with a refrigerator and a sink. Along another wall there was a bunk bed and in the middle of the room was a large table with six chairs around it. Along another wall were shelves with books on them and places to hang clothes. In the corner was a door. "Bathroom and shower there," Bob pointed. Over the sink was a large window that looked out into a field bordered by cottonwood trees on one side. "You can stay here. Pay is four hundred a month, room and board. You can eat breakfast and dinner with the missus and me. Lunch, you get in the field. I'll pay you cash if you don't want to tell the government and I don't care what your name is. Or I'll pay you a check if you want to claim it."

"Cash," I said.

"Good. You start tomorrow. You can take today and look around the place. See where everything is. Look at tractors and everything. If you want, there's some fishing poles in the corner of the barn. Little creek you saw walking up here is full of brookies." He pointed to the sink. "Under the sink is pots and pans and grease and things like that are in the cupboard. No drinking during the day. No getting drunk on my place anytime. No cussing around my wife." He looked at me once again as he was leaving. "Small world," and he laughed his deep laugh.

I unpacked my suitcase, stacking my clothes on the shelf. In the bathroom I put the remains of the scented soap by the Ivory and the Lava that were in the soap dish. There were a dozen large towels. I put a towel by the sink and took out a skillet and coffeepot from underneath and laid them by the sink. In the cupboard was coffee and jelly, ketchup, sugar and non-dairy creamer.

As I sat at the table looking out the window I felt I could live there forever. I went outside and walked towards the barn, feeling fortunate to have landed such a good job. In the barn, Bob was looking at sacks of seed. The barn was as neat as the outside of the place. Along one wall was a large bench with tools. Along another, rows of oil barrels and grease. In the corner were the sacks of seeds. Bob looked at me. "There's some overalls over there. Pick out a pair. No need to ruin good clothes working." He looked at my boots. "Plus, I got some old boots I'll bring over for you. You seem to have about the same size foot as my son." I noted a tinge of sadness in his voice at the mention of his son. In the far corner I could see the fishing poles. Bob turned away from me and I looked at them. There were six poles, all with cheap spinning reels filled with mono line. On a small shelf were hooks and sinkers and several coffee cans with plastic lids with holes aready in them, for worms, and two creels. A foot away was a shovel. Bob laughed, his laugh echoing off the metal sides of the barn. "Worms all around the fence around the corral.''

I took the shovel and can and went outside and off behind the barn to the corrals I hadn't seen walking in. Within ten minutes I had a dozen nice fat worms. Back in the barn Bob was gone. I picked out a pole, grabbed some hooks and lead weights, a creel and cut out across the field towards the stream. As I walked through the field I looked back and saw a woman taking laundry off the line. She waved at me and I waved back. I wished Barbara was with me here, walking across the field. I wished I could show her the sky and the black birds and the horses in the distance. I wished I could take her hand and say,''See? See, this is what life is. It's these tiny moments when you don't have to make sense. It's these seconds and minutes when the earth and the sky and your heart all seem to be one.'' I stopped and looked at the horizon. I was alone but I did not feel alone.

I crept up to the stream, feeling like an Indian or a small boy. There were no trophies in that water. I didn't have an L.L. Bean bamboo rod or custom-tied flies. I had a cheap rod and a worm dangling from the end.

The water was icy and clear. The brown rocks on the bottom looked like a mosaic. I tossed the worm into a small riffle that flowed into a pool not more than three feet across and two feet deep. As the worm tumbled into the pool a silver flash grabbed it and in my excitement the first fish sailed over my head into the grass behind me. I pounced on him like a bear grabbing his first salmon of the season and as I held him I did not see the tiny red and yellow spots running down his side. I didn't see the sun glisten off of his body. I saw him brown and crispy on my plate as I shook salt over him. I caught four trout out of that pool and moved to the next. Within an hour I had a dozen. A great meal for one man. I sat down by the stream and laid them out on the grass. The largest first, second largest second, and on down the line.

Once again I wished Barbara was there. There to see the green grass by the stream side with twelve trout all in a neat row. There to listen to the water gurgle over the rocks. I felt like a small child who had found a shiny rock to take back to his mother. To him the rock is a diamond. When you are little you can give presents like that and not feel inadequate or that the gift isn't enough or that the gift isn't enough or expensive enough. When you're little a gift can be just a gift.

As I walked back to the cabin I felt I had lived there forever and

I had fished the creek since I was a boy. I stood the pole by the door of the cabin and went inside. There was a knife under the sink. Outside two large cats were looking at my creel hanging from a nail. They followed me out behind the barn, tails up and meowing, telling me how much they loved me. Both cats sat devouring the fish guts and heads. With the fish clean they followed me back to the house and came inside. One went straight to the bed and the other one jumped up to the window sill.

Coffee was brewing on the stove when I heard a knock on the door. I answered it and a woman was standing there. She was tall and proud looking. Her unmade up face seemed pure. "Frank," she spoke. "I'm Bob's wife, Mary."

"Come in," I said feeling stupid, asking the person who owned the house to come in. She had a paper sack in her arm. "I saw you fishing." She set the sack down on the table. "Here's some flour, salt, pepper, some frozen juice, milk, loaf of bread and some canned vegetables. I figured you might like to eat your trout tonight and not eat with us."

"Thank you. I feel like it's Christmas."

"Next time you go, catch me a batch too, would you? I love trout but Bob doesn't like them and he doesn't fish."

"I will. How many do you want?"

"Four or five is enough for me. See you've made a couple of friends." She looked at the cats who were asleep.

She walked to the door and I followed her trying to think of something to say but there was nothing that came to my mind. She stood on the porch and looked at the fishing pole. "That was my son's," she said smiling. She moved a strand of her hair out of her eye. "I hope you like it here." And she walked off.

I ate all the fish for dinner with a can of corn. When it was dark I took a chair out to the porch and sat down. I noticed a pair of worn work boots and overalls by the door.

The night sky was cloudless. It was one of those nights when the Milky Way seemed to cover the whole sky. A chorus of cricket chirps came from the fields and one of the dogs occasionally let out a low bark but it was not a bark of alarm. I saw a light on at Bob's house.

When I was young and my parents would take us to see their folks, every evening after dinner all the grownups would go sit on the porch. There was a swing and several old rocking chairs. They would sit in the dark and talk grownup talk and watch people walk by and say hello to the dark forms. After a child was ready for bed he could go out on the porch and sit on the step, if he or she was quiet, and listen to the slow even noise of the swing and rocking chairs. The swing squeaked as it swung back and each of the chairs had a particular sound. They sounded like heartbeats. Everyone had his own chair and nobody else ever sat in anyone else's chair. The swing was reserved for company. There was no radio blaring, no television. Just the sounds of the swing and the crickets and the heartbeat of the chairs intermingled with talk. On those visits my grandparents and parents talked about time mostly. What happened when they were young and where different people in town had gone off to. It was a secure feeling to sit on the step and watch an occasional toad hop across the porch and listen to history. We have lost a lot, now that we have quit building houses with porches. People sit around the television or VCR and try to ignore life. I knew why my great-grandmother died and how she lived although I never saw her. I knew about uncles in the Civil War and old love affairs of relatives that could be mentioned because they were dead and it was no longer shameful now that it was history. I distinctly remember the night when I discovered that my mother had had a boyfriend beside my father when they were in high school. I laid in bed that night listening to the breeze rustle the oak leaves outside the window and thought about the other boyfriend my mother almost married and wondered what I might have been.

The light in Bob's house went out. I was sitting in a ranch in Montana covered by the stars, getting ready to get up early in the morning and start work. I wished I could get up, go inside and find Barbara sitting in her chair reading and ask her to come out and sit on the porch with me. We wouldn't have to talk. We would just sit there and be together for a while and then we would get up. I would hold the door open for her and we would go to sleep. Just before falling asleep I would kiss her on the nose and tell her I loved her and in the dark I would know she was smiling.

Somewhere in the distance a pack of coyotes began to howl and the dogs, one by one, joined in the chorus.

CHAPTER VI

"Up and at 'em," Bob hollered through the window. I jumped out of bed as though it was an attack. It took me a moment to realize where I was. "Breakfast in fifteen minutes," came through the dark and I heard his laughter and the fading sound of his footsteps. I turned on the light, brushed my teeth quickly, ran a comb through my hair and put on my clothes. As I walked towards the light of their house I could not see the faintest hint of sun on the horizon. The back door to the main house was open and I could see Bob sitting at a large table through the screen door. I knocked. "Come on in." I went directly into the large kitchen. The table could have easily held eight men. Mary poured me coffee and smiled.

"What time is it," I mumbled after taking a sip of coffee.

"Four-thirty," Bob spoke to the paper.

As soon as the cup was empty it was full again and after two cups I felt awake. Mary saw the life in my face. "It'll take a few days to get used to the hours." She put a plate of ham and eggs and toast in front of me. Then she set down a plate of hot cakes. Bob was not eating. "Aren't you going to eat?" I asked.

Bob laughed. "I already ate."

I ate the food and drank more coffee. When the coffee was settling the food I looked out the window and could see a faint dash of red over the mountain. "That was good, thank you Mary." Mary had not sat down since I had been in the kitchen but then she did and spoke. "The sunrise is so beautiful. It's the best part of the day. Everything is so fresh. Each and every day brings a new start, a new chance at it all." Bob reached over with his large and weather-beaten hand and touched her on the cheek gently. "Lady," he smiled, "There is nothing prettier than you in the morning."

I felt as though I was invading something I should not see but the feel of their love filled the room along with the smell of ham and hot cakes and coffee. Mary took his hand from her face, held it and laughed. "You old dog," she chided. "You know how to keep me getting up at this hour to cook your breakfast."

Bob stood up and looked at me. "Well, you ready?"

I nodded my head. "Thanks again for the food, Mary." By the door was my lunch and a one gallon jug filled with water. I followed Bob to his Ford pickup. We went out through the main entrance to the house and turned left on a dirt road. After about twenty minutes of listening to the farm report and the weather on the radio, Bob stopped the truck. On the edge of a field sat a tractor with a set of discs attached. "Here she is." The field was a rolling field partially climbing up a slight mountain, or mole hill as they call rises where there are real mountains. It was covered with stubble from the last fall's wheat. "I want to disc this stubble in. Shouldn't take more than a week. By the gate into the field is a tank filled with diesel fuel and a barrel of oil and a grease gun. Can you handle it?"

"Shouldn't be any problem."

"All right. Good luck."

I got out of the truck and Bob drove off. He wasn't going to check on me or anything. If I couldn't handle it I guess I would just pack my bag and go.

It was six when I started the tractor after checking all the oil levels. It was seven after my first pass around the edge of the field. It felt good. The steady sound of the tractor, the disc blades cutting into the earth. The sound of the wheat stubble as it cracked and folded into the ground. I looked around me and it was like riding around in the middle of a postcard. One of those cards you send relatives telling them to eat their heart out while you're on vacation. With each pass I looked at my watch and my lunch sitting by the diesel tank. Two passes and it was only eight o'clock. I had four hours until lunch.

It was twelve fifteen when I stopped the tractor by the gas tank and shut the engine. I gassed Betty, my name for the tractor, and then sat down for lunch. I opened the brown sack and had two lunch meat sandwiches with lettuce and tomato, a bag of Fritos, an orange and a banana. With the lunch finished, I got back on Betty and started off again. I was halfway around the field when the bliss I had felt for the day suddenly disappeared with the realization that I would not be here long. I was just a temporary stop on this ranch. I was oblivious to the tractor and the field and the cloud of dirt I rode in for the rest of the day. I was on the far side of the field and it was growing dark when I saw Bob's pickup truck stop by the gate. Twenty minutes later I pulled up to the tank and shut off the engine. I refueled Betty, checked all the oil and greased her before walking to the truck. Bob smiled as I got in. "How was it?" Seeing his smile I tried to feel better. "Fine. Tractor is running good."

As we rode back to the ranch house in the dark we listened to country and western music on the radio. Back at the headquarters I started to walk towards the bunk house. "Dinner in thirty minutes. Soon as you clean up, come on over."

As I stood in the shower I watched the brown dirt swirl down the drain and thought of the green air of LA.

We had pork chops, corn, salad, wheat bread, milk, coffee and apple pie for dinner. As soon as I was done I stood up and carried my dishes to the sink. Mary looked as fresh as she had that morning. "Here," she said. "Take this." She handed me another piece of pie on a plate to take back to the bunkhouse with me. "Thank you."

"Same time in the morning, Frank," Bob told me. As I walked back to the cabin the dogs followed me smelling the pie and wagging their tails.

I put the pie in the refrigerator and fell into bed, gazing out the window at the stars and wishing I could stay here.

The week passed quickly. Breakfast, lunch, dinner, bed. It was Saturday night and I didn't even know it. Bob spoke after dinner, "No work tomorrow. Start again Monday."

Mary looked at me. "Maybe if you want, you can catch us a batch of trout and I'll cook them up for lunch tomorrow."

"I'll do that." As I was leaving I looked back at Mary and Bob sitting at the table. "I really want to thank you two for treating me so well. I appreciate it." Bob looked confused and Mary smiled an understanding smile almost like the smiles my grandmother used to give me. "You're a nice man, Frank. Remember that."

Two of the dogs joined me as I sat on the porch. They sat on their haunches looking into the darkness, occasionally moving their heads slowly. I reached out and scratched one behind the ears and heard his tail thump on the wooden floor. "I'll catch you some trout, lady. It will be my pleasure."

The morning was another beautiful day. I woke up before the sun, conditioned by then, drank some coffee and was digging worms by the time the sky was purple. As the sun was clearing the horizon I was standing by a stream and by nine I had fifteen brookies. They were cleaned and in the refrigerator by ten. At noon I took them over to Mary when I saw her moving around in the kitchen. "Come in, Frank," she spoke before I could knock.

She was pleased when I showed her the trout. "I haven't eaten any trout since . . ." and her voice trailed off and she looked at me for a moment. "Since Bill was killed." I could feel her pain but there was nothing to say. "You were in the army, weren't you Frank?"

I nodded my head and then asked, "How did you know?"

"You were in Vietnam. I can see it in your eyes. All you boys have that look. My son died over there."

"I'm sorry," I said but it sounded feeble.

"You remind me a lot of him. Quiet. Looking. Looking for something. Something you really don't know what it is but it's a feeling that never goes away." Mary took the trout and ran water over them and put them on a plate. "You need a lady, Frank."

"You sound like my mother," I answered. "A good women is the answer to everything."

Mary turned and pointed her finger at me. "It is, young man. And don't you ever think it isn't. A good woman will help you get through this life and you will help her. Sit down, Frank. Want some coffee?" I didn't want any coffee but I didn't want to leave either so I said yes.

"You're lost Frank. I can see it on your face. Something terrible is eating at you." Now I wanted to get up and leave but I couldn't. "But Frank," she continued, "You just hang in there. It will all come together one day."

"My grandmother told me that when I saw her, Mary. Sometimes I wonder."

"You have a girl somewhere, Frank?"

"Sure do," I said matter-of-factly but then I remembered maybe it was only in my mind.

"Well, you should get back to that lady as soon as you can." I wanted to tell her I couldn't. I wanted to tell her there was a fire in me, I wanted to tell her I needed to find something to believe in. I wanted to tell her I felt cheated by the country, lied to, used. But I couldn't. "I bet she is pretty and I bet she is blonde."

"How did you know?"

"I don't know, just seems to me you would like blondes." Mary poured flour in a bowl and put the fish in the flour. Then she put bacon grease in a frying pan and put it on the stove. "Did my boy die for nothing, Frank?" she asked with her back to me.

I wanted to tell her no with the feeling I had in my body. I wanted to tell her no because I love my father and mother and used to love my country but I bowed my head and looked into my coffee cup.

"We were all so young, Mary, when we went. Young and filled with ideas of freedom and honor, thinking we were going to help. America and pride. He died because he was brave and he believed in the country, Mary." And then I thought about Bill, the truck driver. "He wasn't a hypocrite, Mary. You should be proud."

Mary turned and looked at me. Her face was filled with pain but there were no more tears. She had cried enough. "When he died, I quit believing, Frank."

I stood up and walked over to her and we hugged each other, unspeaking, and then pulled apart.

"That's why you're bumming around the country, Frank. You don't know either, do you?"

"No, Mary, I don't know. And until I do, I'm not worth a damn to anybody, especially some pretty lady who, for some reason, I love dearly.

Mary took a deep breath. "Well, then, we do know one thing."

"What's that?"

"You and I are going to sit here and eat all these trout and drink a couple of cold beers."

"Bob said no drinking around here, Mary."

Mary laughed a jovial, happy laugh. "Son, Bob can tell anybody on this place what to do but if I say you can drink a few beers with me, then you can drink a few beers with me."

"Okay, by God, where are they?"

"You sit down over here." Mary went to the refrigerator and pulled out two long neck Coors, opened them and set one down for me. I picked it up.

"Here's to life, Frank. Life and whatever it may bring."

"You have a beautiful heart, Mary," I told her and took a swig.

Mary set her beer down. "You should let that little lady you love so much decide if she can put up with you, confused or not. Ever think about that?"

I shook my head. "No, I never thought about that."

"What is life, without love, Frank? Money, possessions? It's nothing without love. Nothing." She turned down the fire under the grease and put a fish in the pan. It popped and she put in more. "And let me tell you. Love together is far better than love apart. There is a point where that absence makes the heart grow fonder is a bunch of bull."

Before I knew it she was sitting down with a platter of trout and two more beers. We had each eaten a trout when Bob walked in. He looked at the beer in front of us, looked at me, looked at his wife and walked over to the refrigerator and got himself a beer. Sitting down he laughed. "What's the party about?"

Mary sipped the beer and winked at me. "Love. The party's about love."

"Well, hell." Bob looked serious. "I wish I had gotten here sooner."

"Want a trout?" Mary spoke pointing at the fish.

"You know I hate fish."

"I know. Just thought I'd ask."

Bob leaned over and kissed his wife on the forehead. "Lady, you are the rose of my life."

Mary looked at him seriously. "And you are the only thorn I could ever take."

Bob looked at me. "She gets brave when she's had a few beers."

When the fish were all gone Bob decided Mary and I each needed another beer to wash them down with and Bob needed a beer because he had to watch us eat fish. When my beer was finished I stood up from the table. "Thanks for everything, but three beers is about enough for me."

Mary walked me to the door. "You write that little lady, Frank."

I felt stupid. "I don't have a pen or paper, beside not having envelopes or stamps."

"Frank, you should be ashamed of yourself. Even that old cowboy wrote me when he was away in the army. Everyday."

"I'll get some when I get paid," I said. "I promise."

"Good."

The dogs were sleeping in the yard and didn't even bother to get up when I walked by. I was part of the family now.

Back in the cabin I took the books down from the shelf, put them on the table and sat down. There were four battered westerns but they didn't draw my attention I wished I had had a pen and paper. I would have written Barbara. I should have written my folks too. I had not written them a word since my release from prison. I went outside feeling restless and looked at the stars. The stars are nothing to look at while confused. Small concepts like infinity and millions of light years and life on other planets does not help to uncloud the mind. I sat down on the porch and heard a dog walk over to me and sit beside me. Dogs have a way of knowing if someone wants company. He poked his cold nose into my hand as if to say, ''Pat me. It will make you feel better.'' It was the big dog that tore at me when I first walked down the road. Even mean things need pats. I wondered about Mary's son Bill. I thought about her statement that he was a lot like me. I wondered if he watched all the Audie Murphy and John Wayne movies and thought war was a glorious calling. I wondered if he was filled with honor and love for his country. If he thought he could do no wrong and God truly was on our side. I might have even seen him during my time in the army and didn't even know it. If he was killed, then he was in infantry and trained in Fort Polk or California. He might have been in one of those bars filled with whores we used to go to feeling tough and alone. We might have taken the same girl back to her dirty little room behind the bar for fifteen minutes of cheap sex. Maybe he was the lucky one now. He was dead. He did not have to wait anymore for the unavoidable. He did not have to question or search for meaning. For him it was over. Pain was for the living. Pain was the sight of a face that could cry no longer but could never forget.

I glanced at the dog by my feet and at the dark boots sitting beside the door. Those and the fishing pole standing against the wall were Bill's. It did not bother me to work in a dead man's boots. Life was for living. It went on. The light in the kitchen went out and I could visualize Bob and Mary walking to their bedroom. I wondered what they were talking about or if they mentioned me. I went back inside and held the door open for the dog to come in. He hesitated for a moment deciding if he wanted to give up his freedom of the outdoors for a night inside but then he gingerly entered the room and looked around before lying down on the throw rug in front of the sink. I turned off the light and lay down on my bed. I did not feel happy but I did not feel bad. I hoped Barbara missed me and as sleep covered me I wished I was rich. Then I could have been one of those bored people who sit around drinking, telling people his problems and they all listen because he is rich. I didn't know what time it was but it was early and still dark. The dog was scratching at the door wanting out. I stumbled over and let the dog out and turned on the light. It was two AM. I turned the light off and laid back down. I did not feel the least bit sleepy. I wished I had writing material, I would have written Barbara. It had only been ten or eleven days since I had left LA but it seemed I had been traveling for years. The dog scratched at the door to get back in but I did not get up. That's how it was in life. You give somebody a break once and they try to take advantage of you. I laughed at the raw wit, trying not to believe it but as sleep came over me once again I felt it was probably true.

The next day after work when I came into the cabin there was a stack of typing paper on the desk with envelopes and two pens. Seeing them made me feel good inside. After dinner as I was leaving the kitchen, Mary handed me a book of stamps. ''You write,'' she said simply and turned her back on me to start the dishes before I could say anything.

Back at the cabin I sat down and wrote on a sheet of paper: Dear Barbara.

Then my mind went blank. All of the feelings I felt for her, all of the moments spent wishing she was with me, I could not put into words. Where to start, what to say?

Hi, remember me? I'm the guy you let stay at your place and we thought we were falling in love and after you let me into your bed I took off like a scared rabbit.

After several minutes of indecision I began.

I am sorry I have not written sooner but I did not have paperand pen. Good excuse, huh? After you let me off beside the highway I caught a ride with a truck driver all the way to Seattle. It was a good ride. Then I hung around for a while and now I am in Bozeman, Montana, driving a tractor on a ranch to make a few more dollars before moving on.

I took the sheet of paper and wadded it into a ball and threw it in the general direction of the sack I used for a garbage can by the sink. I began again.

Dear Lady,

There have been many nights I wished I could sit by a fire with you like we did beside the highway. I wish I could see your smile and tell you face to face about my journey and all the people I have met. I see things along my trip and I want you here to see them with me. I do something and I wish I could tell you about it. But I find it impossible to sit here and tell you in words all of the feelings I have felt for the last few weeks. I have used up all of the bar of soap you gave me. Strange thing to feel sad about but it made me sad. I hope all is going well for you and you do not forget me. You are like a warm blanket on a cold night.

I signed the letter simply, Frank.

The next morning before breakfast I walked up the driveway to the mailbox and put the letter in. "Did you write?" Mary asked me before I sat down to eat.

"Sure did," I answered.

"Good." she replied.

"Write who?" Bob asked..

Mary filled his coffee cup. "I don't remember talking to you." Bob laughed and didn't say anymore.

Riding out to the field Bob was talkative. "Mary told me you were a vet. Said she talked to you about our son." Bob's voice was still jovial. "A woman carries her pain longer than a man. A man can understand dying in a war. It's just part of being a man in this world. You don't weigh the right or wrong of it. It just is. You proud you went, Frank?"

I wished I was already on the tractor listening to the throb of the engine and the crackle of the wheat stubble. "I was proud," I answered truthfully.

Bob looked at me hearing more than the words in my voice. "Let it be, son. Just let it be and get on with your life. More people than you boys been fucked around. You have to hitch up your pants and go on. Sometimes it isn't the easiest thing but you just have to go on." He stopped the truck by the gate to the field. The tractor waited for me like a trusted old friend. As I got out of the truck I told Bob, "Thanks."

When Bob returned at dusk the field was done. I had wiped the dirt and grime off the engine and topped off the gas and oil. It was a good feeling to look at the field and see it completed. A passing of time going round and round and round. It was like life, I hoped. If you just keep going round and round, one day you would reach a point where you didn't have to keep going around. You would get somewhere and at the somewhere, it would be okay.

That night at dinner I looked at Bob and Mary and spoke. "You folks have been very good to me. Feeding me and everything. Letting me fish your stream. It's been nice being here. I haven't spent time alone for a while. You make yourself alone but you are not alone. Outdoors with the stars and the sky and the mountains one can be alone. But I have to be on my way."

"You going back to that girl, Frank?" Mary asked.

"No, not yet. She might not even want to see me now."

"Why don't you call her, Frank?"

"I can't." I felt cornered.

"Well, Frank," Bob spoke. "You're a good worker and I want you to know that if you ever need a job, you can always come back here."

"Thank you, Bob. That's good of you."

Bob left the room and came back handing me an evelope. "Here's your pay."

I walked out into the night, not really wanting to leave the kitchen. I wanted to stay and smell the odor of food and coffee. I wanted to stay and talk to Mary about fishing and flowers and letters. All of the dogs were on the porch of the cabin. Word had gotten out that I had let one in one night. "You mangy bums," I taunted them. "I know Bob never lets any of you in the house." They all wagged their tails and played stupid. Dogs have a way of playing stupid when they need to. I let them all in and sat at the table watching as they felt nervous and could not get comfortable. When I opened the door they ran over each other to get out.

In the morning I packed my suitcase and put the pots and pans back under the sink. I looked around the cabin and then outside into the field where the tiny stream ran and the brook trout waited to be caught and rolled in flour and fried. As I walked towards the gravel road, Mary called to me from the front door of the house. She walked out to me with a brown sack. "Here's a little food." She handed me the bag. I smiled at her and she smiled back. "Good luck in your life. Frank."

"Thank you for everything, Mary." We both turned at the same time.

A few hours later I stopped walking beside the paved highway. I had not even stuck out my thumb. As I stood there an old truck screeched on its brakes and stopped. It was Kate, who first gave me a ride to Bob's. "Bob work you too hard?" she bellowed.

I laughed. She still had a pack of cigarettes in her shirt. "Nope, just time to get going, is all."

"Where are you going?"

"Down the highway."

"Well, hop in. I'm going about ninety miles to look at some hay."

I slammed the door behind me. I remembered the envelope with my pay in it stuck in my jacket pocket and opened it. There was four hundred dollars. Way too much.

"Good old cash money," Kate bellowed. "I'm surprised that skinflint even payed you."

"They were good to me."

"Bob's a good man. He's my brother."

I looked at her and laughed. "Well, next time you see your brother, you tell him thank you for me, okay?"

Kate fiddled in her pocket for her cigarettes. "Next time I see him will be Christmas. He and I find it much easier to get along when we only see each other during the holidays. He never did like the man I married." Then she laughed her deep laugh and it sounded like Bob. "But I told him he didn't have to sleep with the bastard, I did." We both laughed. There was a little bit of heaven riding down the highway in the old pickup with the dust billowing around my face and the exhaust so loud I had to holler to speak. Life seemed a little bit better because of old trucks.

We must have gone the ninety miles because Kate slammed on the brakes. "I go that way, son," and she pointed up a gravel road." Custer is only a few miles down the road. Bus runs through there and you can get a room for the night."

"What night is it?" I asked.

"Saturday. Stay out of the dance halls. These small town cowboys don't like strangers messing with their women."

"Thanks for the ride and the advice.' Once again in my life I watched the truck sputter off.

Custer was like any western town. It could have been picked up and placed in Idaho or North Dakota, Wyoming, New Mexico, or Colorado. There was a main street about five blocks long and several small streets running in either direction. On the main street was the courthouse with police cars parked on the side, the grocery store, several small cafes, two bars, and a small motel with tiny rooms. The room was clean, the rug blue to match the bedspread. The shower curtain was yellow and the water pressure poor from the build up of lime on the shower head. I hated to think what the water did to a person's insides. The man who ran the motel lived in a trailer out back. Even he didn't want to live in one of the rooms. By the time I had registered, I knew his history. "If I had money, I'd get out of this cold son of a bitch," he told me. "Hot in the summer. Bugs. Cold in the winter. Cold as hell. If I had any money I'd go live in Hawaii or something. Somewhere where I could lay on the beach and look at all those pretty girls. Couldn't do nothing about it but I'd sure look. Ain't nothing in this country but cows and horses. I've been here my whole life. Used to be a cowboy. Thought it was good. Ride a horse, punch cows, roll cigarettes, spend my money getting drunk and laying some bar whore. Hell. What the hell do I know? So you do what I tell you, son. Get to some warm climate, go somewhere where the women don't wear too many clothes. It's cheaper." He chuckled. "Can't recommend anything in town. Cafes are both the same. Same man owns them. Bars are okay but aren't any hot women around here, just a bunch of cowboys going to get drunk tonight and wish they were somewhere they could get some easy tail."

After taking a shower I looked in the brown sack Mary had given me. There was a steak sandwich and an apple. I felt rich. I had over six hundred dollars to my name. I had not had this much money in over five years.

I turned on the television and watched some cop show. Police are necessary and all that but I still don't like them. Everybody has to hate something, I suppose. I always wondered to myself who would ever be a cop. I put them in the same class as undertakers and lawyers and doctors. When the show was over there was a knock on the door. It was the motel owner.

"Want to have a few beers?" he asked. He had taken a shower and had on a clean shirt and levis. I really didn't pay any attention to him when I was registering. He was in his sixties, his face wrinkled heavily, fingers bent and twisted and a piece of his right ear was missing in a perfect half circle. He noticed me looking at his ear. "Got bit off in a fight years ago. Hurt like hell but didn't bleed much."

I picked up my jacket and we walked down to the bar. I felt like I was taking my life in my own hands. "No Knives Or Guns Inside" was written on the door of the bar. I wondered if I was really brave. Music was blaring through the door and there were atleast twenty pickups lined up outside. Inside one could hardly see because of the smoke. There were two pool tables with quarters lined up around the edge and several tables around a dance floor no more than ten by ten feet. The bar running down the right side had no stools and there was no room to squeeze in between the cowboys.

Two cowboys were dancing with women who looked like they could bite your head off and spit it across the room. Everyone of the cowboys looked snockered and they were all talking loud enough to be heard above the music. All of them made comments to the hotel owner. "Come to join the living, Slim?" Slim smiled at them and shook hands with a few. I didn't know why he wanted me to come with him. It looked as though there was more than enough company for a few beers.

"What do you want?" Slim hollered over the music.

"Coors, Coors is fine."

He got four Coors and carried them by the necks over to a small shelf running along the wall. We set two of the beers down and held the others and watched the cowboys put their egos out on the pool game. There were spittoons scattered all over the bar and most were used frequently.

"Saturday night in shit town." Slim hollered and drank his beer. It was ten o'clock by the Budweiser clock over the bar when the place erupted. I was watching one of the women dance with another cowboy when I heard the sound of fist against face. The next thing I knew there were fists and boots and beer bottles going everywhere. I caught a quick shot in the stomach and one to the forehead. Slim was hollering and laughing and cussing all at the same time. I saw him crack a young cowboy across the face with a beer bottle and then grab a pool cue and lay into another one. Feeling blood run down my face, I punched out at the next face before me and then at another.

Then there was the sound of two pistol shots and the bar was instantly quiet. Punches half-thrown stopped. The bartender held the pistol still pointed at the ceiling. Two cowboys were still dancing with the women, unaffected by the excitment.

"All right, you assholes," the bartender hollered. "Everybody dig into those levis and put some money in that hat Leroy here is going to take around for all the damage. And then let's get back to having a lonely but good time." Everybody dusted themselves off and smiled to whoever they were about to punch and put whatever they could in the hat. When the hat was back at the bar the bartender looked at the pile of money. "This round is on me but the next fucker who starts any trouble has me to tangle with." Within a minute the pool game was back on and everything was back to normal. Slim grinned at me and I noticed for the first time that he had very few teeth in his mouth. "See what I mean? Fucking town!" I shook my head and made my way out of the bar, taking pains not to bump into anyone. The motel bed felt fine. My ears rang from the juke box. "Dear Barbara," I thought before sleep. "Tonight I almost ended my search. It would have been a befitting end, dead before there were any answers. Maybe just as well."

During the night I dreamed I was standing in the shower with Barbara and I was rubbing a bar of scented soap over her back. She was speaking, "At the office today they tried to tell me I wasn't going to get a raise because I hadn't been there long enough. I told them I should get as much as any man. You know, the boss just laughed." She turned, her face red with anger. I pulled her to me and the hot water ran over both of us. "I like you when you're angry," I spoke. She pushed back from me. "Are you listening or not?" Then with a pause we both laughed.

In the morning my forehead hurt and there was a large bump on my shin. Outside the street was deserted except for three trucks in front of the closest cafe. I went back into the room, washed up and headed for breakfast. Inside the cafe two cowboys sat with the ladies from the bar. They were not talking and looked as though they had not slept for weeks. The sun was up and the magic was gone. I sat at the counter on a round soda fountain stool. The man who was the bartender at the bar was behind the counter. It was a small town. I thought about what Slim said, living in a place where the women don't wear many clothes and it's warm all the time.

I was half way done with my pancakes when Slim came in. He looked as though he had never rested better. "Boys," he said to the cowboys with the women. "Casey," he smiled at the bartender turned restauranter.

Casey nodded his head. "A little exciting last night," he commented.

Slim agreed. "Yeah but not out of hand. I'll have the usual."

Slim ate two eggs over easy swimming in tabasco sauce and a cup of coffee.

"Where do you catch the bus around here?" I asked Slim.

"Right here. This is the bus stop. Only thing that keeps this cafe alive."

"Where do you want to go?" Casey asked.

"Denver," I heard myself say.

"Forty-two dollars and you can be on your way in two hours." I gave him my money and he gave me a ticket he made out by the cash register. "Bus leaves here at eleven-fifteen. More coffee?"

I drank another cup, paid my check and left. As I stood outside the cafe I wondered if Barbara would like to move to Hawaii and start all over.

Two hours later when the bus came I was the only passenger. The bus driver ignored me as I got on. It was okay. My forehead was hurting and I didn't like the way he looked anyway.

CHAPTER VII

I didn't know if it was fourteen or twenty-four hours later that we arrived in Denver. Four bus changes, one flat tire and two breakdowns beside desolate rural roads left me on a plane monks try to reach. But it was nice being in no rush. Looking for oneself is not like rushing off to work everyday and rushing through the week to Friday so you can rest. When one has gone through life as long as I have, there is no need to rush. It all seems to be the same time no matter what one does.

Leaving Montana we had gone through the mountains and then down into the sagebrush covered plains of Wyoming. Then back up into the mountains and over the top into Denver. I could picture the first wagon trains west as they came out of the flat lands of Kansas and saw the Rockies looming over them. The meek stopped and started Denver. The brave went on not because they wanted to but because the damn mountain was there and something inside told them they were stupid to go on but they must.

Denver was just another big city. Filled with people who hate pollution but pollute. They talk about overcrowding yet build more suburbs. People cram into bars each night to try to become something that their forefathers knew was over the mountains. It was depressing to know that in every state there was a version of New York and LA. Some form of consciousness that makes mankind want to pile on top of each other. IBM and Ma Bell might have something to do with the propaganda but that would be hard to prove. I guess the enticement of paid vacations makes one stay in the city. But I would live in LA with Barbara so paid vacations and love, I'll add, would make one stay.

The bus station in Denver made me wish I had a machine gun. With it I could have dashed several hundred yards to a neutral zone without being cut down by muggers. Since I didn't have one I had to walk slowly as though I was not afraid of the menacing looking people on the street and hope I picked the right direction and was not walking deeper into the war zone. I have always had a strange feeling seeing poor destitute people. Without the poor there would be no rich people. It's a national disgrace, the poor. No wonder the nation is dying or gasping for another try. It was a day of disillusionment for me when I realized this country did not take care of its people. Raised with the thought of Lincoln and Washington and for the people and of the people, I thought it was all true. But it was later in life that I realized there were very few people like Bill, the truck driver, who will help a man up. It seems so easy but I suppose greed gets in the way to ruin helping. Cut a floor off a skyscraper, make a road two inches narrower. Tax everything and then forget about income tax. It all seems easy but what do I know? I've never been rich or had the desire to keep people poor. I would like to sit at a cocktail party one day flashing my diamond pinky ring and my smug well-refined look, my wife with her fresh facial and fur coat beside me being oh so chic and made up. I could talk about the oil prices out of the Middle East and the cost of a second home on the island or what vacation out of the three I took this year was the best. Maybe I wouldn't think about the poor man. I wouldn't have to ride buses and see them, I suppose, so I could forget. It is easy to grow bitter at times. A battle I fight constantly, is to try feeling human. I figure if one can take all the injustice of life and inequality and not grow bitter, then that means something. What that something is seems to have slipped my mind but it is something.

Having successfully made my way from the bus station, I felt better. Being killed by a poor person after feeling so empathetic for them some people would call karma but babies die, blowing the hell out of the idea of karma.

I stood on the corner and wondered why in the hell I wanted to come to Denver. There was nothing there that wasn't in Montana and nothing in Montana that wasn't in Seattle. I felt like some stupid puppy running around in circles chasing his tail because it makes the kids laugh. Only the kid in my case was Barbara. Dear Barbara, maybe another night in your bed would have stopped this circle. Maybe another walk on the beach hand in hand or a drive back to the desert when we could fall asleep looking at the stars. Maybe with a few kisses there wouldn't have been veterans and taxes and hospitals and revolution and killing and rape in my mind. Or maybe with Barbara beside me it just wouldn't matter. I could have looked at her and said, ''Lady, hold me and let me hold you. I can't give you anything but my heart but I'm not poor. I'm not a bum sitting by the bus station in any town with stubble on my face and no life in my eyes. I'm just me, just a man, just a thing that, for some reason, was plopped down on the face of this earth. I don't want to be a politican, I don't want two houses, I don't want insurance or to be a movie star. I just want somebody to tell me it's okay, I love you.''

I looked down the street to my left at the infinity of shop lights and people and cars. I looked at my right and saw the same thing. Everywhere were cars and people and stop lights and stores and more cars and more people. I thought there must be another God somewhere. The God of stuff. One is born into this world knowing at infancy what one needs in life. You need food and warmth and love. Then slowly the new god starts to come into your life. One god is saying, ''Thou Shalt Not Kill, Thou Shalt Not Steal.'' This new god says ''Thou Shall Need More And More As You Grow Older. Thou Shall Need Not Ten Dresses But A Hundred. Thou Shall Need Twenty-Five Pair Of Shoes, Two Watches, Sixteen Bracelets, Five Toothbrushes And Thirty Pots and Pans.'' In order to reach heaven, thou shall need stuff. As soon as your garage is full with stuff, you know you are getting close to this god. You have so much stuff you don't even know where to put it so people can see it. And then the Stuff god says, ''thou shall give your stuff to Goodwill so you can buy more stuff." The Stuff god stays up at night and whispers to women while they sleep. "Thou shall want all the stuff thou can possibly talk your idiot husband into wasting his life over." Then he goes to the sleeping man and says, "Thou will get better sex if thou buys the woman more stuff."

Denver, Colorado was doing something to me. It must have been the altitude or the high mountain air that was brown and not green.

I couldn't take it. I turned around and half-ran back to the bus station. I needed to go back to my roots. Back to where I used to go as a child. Back to where my grandparents spent their lives and their parents lived and died. The black man behind the ticket counter looked at me without speaking. Poor people don't have to talk. Talking won't enhance their position in life. "Ticket for Sheldon, Iowa," I told him.

He smiled. "I like Iowa. Was there for several years. Nice dirt. Good black dirt. Grow a lot of food there." He gave me all the tickets with transfers. "Eighty-two bucks, son."

I walked away from the counter holding the tickets and looking at the straight backed seats and pinball machines against the wall. I felt better. Maybe my true calling in life was to live inside a bus station and get out every so often to go to the bathroom, eat junk food, and spit insane ideas and philosophies at the nearest person. I could carry a little box to stand on, have a tin can and a sign saying I was the bus station philospher. Then, when I got famous I could have an assistant that would travel with me, maybe Barbara, who would pass out cards saying: For God's Sake, All he wants you to do is buy stuff.

I walked into the restaurant that was all red plastic-covered seats and neon lights that were more blue than white. Two waitresses walked back and forth behind the counter between four customers. I sat at the end of the counter and a waitress came over to me. She was tall, slim, with dark hair, dark eyes and very little make up. She smiled at me. It was a warm smile, sad at the corners, but warm. I smiled back. Sincere, one of those smiles you can feel in your eyes.

"Listen," she said. "I'm on a break for thirty minutes. Would you like to sit in a booth and have some company?"

I looked at her name tag pinned over her right breast on her blue blouse. "I'd love to, Terry."

She walked around the end of the counter and I followed her to a booth. She slid into one side and I put my suitcase down and slid into the other. I noticed her eyes seemed bothered. "I just need someone to talk to. I don't want to be any bother," she spoke shyly.

"Hey. It's okay. I'd be glad to talk to you."

She smiled a fleeting little girl smile and took a deep breath. "Sometimes it's better to talk to someone you really don't know. Then they won't sit and tell you things just to make you feel better or because they have feelings about everybody involved. What's your name?" she asked.

"Frank."

"Well, Frank, you talk to me and I'll get your dinner."

"No, you smiled big for me and I'll get your dinner." She started to protest but surrendered. "Next time, though, you can buy for you and me."

The other waitress brought over two menus and two glasses of water. "Who's your handsome friend?" Terry made a face and the other waitress walked away. I looked at my menu but stole glances at Terry. I realized she was young, early twenties. I felt sorry for her for an instant. As one grows older one feels sorry for people who are going to have to go through it. When the waitress came back I ordered the special: roast beef, vegetables, salad, coffee and pie. Terry ordered an hamburger. She had seen the special and knew better. The waitress brought my coffee and ignored Terry. The coffee, under the blue neon, looked like everything one could consider evil. I sensed that Terry was searching for ways to begin and I spoke, "I'm a good listener."

She looked deep into my eyes. "I was married a little over a year ago. I was going to college and so was the boy I married. He's still going there and I dropped out to help pay the bills." She took a deep breath. "I just found out he's been sleeping with another girl while I'm at work." Her bottom lip trembled slightly but she held her sob inside.

I sipped the cup of sin and said, for want of anything else, "Do you love him?"

"I want to kill him," she replied. Having been in prison with murderers, I knew she was no killer. I reached over the table and took her hand and held it in mine. "Have you told him?" She slid her hand out of my grasp and put her hands in her lap and shook her head no.

"I take it you really love the guy."

"Unfortunately, yes," she replied.

"Lucky guy," I answered.

The waitress brought the special and the hamburger. As they were set down in front of us I wished I had ordered a hamburger. "Special's lousy," Terry commented. I felt like saying why didn't you tell me but what with her husband maybe right at that moment crawling under the sheets with another woman while she and I are sitting there eating, I didn't say anything. "What would you do, Frank?" she asked taking a bite out of the hamburger I coveted.

"Well," I answered poking the roast beef that looked like another form of sin. "I think if I loved the other person I would tell them I knew what was going on and tell them I loved them and see what would happen. If the other person loved me, it would be worth another try but if not, then it would be just as well to have it over with so I could get into the process of geting over the pain."

Terry took another bite of her hamburger. The cheating did not seem to hurt her appetite. She smiled a deep smile at me. "I thought about that. That is a good idea. It's what I'm going to do."

"Good," I said feeling happy for her and happy I said the right thing.

"But," she added, "I also told myself something else." She put her hamburger down and looked at me with searching eyes. "I also said I was going to ask the next good-looking guy I saw if he wanted to go to bed with me." My roast beef looking like sin was not as bad as the coffee so I took a bite. "So?" she stared.

"So?" I replied.

"So, do you want to?"

I swallowed the roast beef and tried to make a joke. "Stand up and slowly turn for me."

She obediently slid out of the booth, looked at me and turned slowly. Her legs were lovely, her rear was round and firm. Her waist small and her breast the size of small oranges, just like I like them. Her lips I know would match mine. She slid back into the booth. "I have a bus to catch, Terry."

"When," she asked without batting an eye.

I pulled the tickets from my pocket. "Three-thirty AM." I looked at the clock on the wall. It was six PM. I used to dream I would be driving a car on a trip and I would pick up a lady hitch-hiker who, for the next week, would fuck my brains out. She would be pretty and smart with a body every man would like to get next to and, unlike most women, would like to do it everyday and not just twice a week. I never dreamed I would be picked up in a bus stop by a girl who asked me. Maybe by some lady wanting to sell it but not somebody like this. "Where?" I asked.

"I have a Ford van with a bed in the back and a mirror on the ceiling."

I scratched my head and smiled. "What time do you get off?"

"I am off."

"You mean this isn't your break?"

She laughed. "No stranger, this is your lucky day." I thought of Barbara. I thought of the bed like a flower and the scented soap. I thought about cheap sex with no feeling and I looked at Terry and said, "What are we waiting for?" She ran the tip of her tongue over her lips and answered, "The check." I waved to the waitress, she brought the check. I left ten dollars on the table and Terry and I walked out. As we walked through the bus station Terry took my hand. "This will be fun." Across the street was the blue Ford van with tinted windows. She unlocked her door and once inside let me in. We drove down the road and she turned on the radio, pushed a few buttons and then turned it off. Making several more turns we were by a park surrounded by street lights. Terry stopped the van and turned off the lights. Locking her door she crawled over the seat. I locked my door and followed her. With both of us in the back she pulled a curtain shut behind the seats and flicked on a dim overhead lamp by the mirror. We were sitting on a mattress covered with a soft blanket. She unzipped her dress and pulled it over her head. She was not wearing a bra or underpants. In the dim light she was beautiful. "Your turn," she giggled. I got out of my clothes and we sat looking at each other. I leaned over and we kissed tenderly. Her tongue searched for the inside of my mouth and my hands ran up her sides and cupped her breasts. Her nipples stood for my touch and grew hard. She pulled me back onto the mattress and whispered. "Take your time. We have until early morning." Her hands ran down my back and she began to moan softly.

It was three AM when Terry stopped in front of the bus station. "Good luck in your life, Frank," she said touching me gently on the cheek. I got out with my suitcase and stood with the door open. "Good luck with your marriage." She smiled, "It will be a lot easier forgiving him knowing we are even." We both laughed as I shut the door. I did not watch her drive away.

Inside the bus station there were several bums trying to sleep on the benches. I went to the restroom, brushed my teeth and washed my face. The bus was called. As I sat on the bus I watched Denver pass by from the freeway and I was content. It wasn't love but it wasn't bad. When all the city lights were gone and there was nothing but darkness outside my window, I shut my eyes. I would wake up somewhere in Kansas and the perfume from Terry's body would still be faintly around me. Life was filled with surprises. One never really knew. I had been asleep for a moment when my head jerked up. Barbara's face was before me and she was saying. "You jerk. You no good jerk." She was scowling. "But I'm not married," I pleaded. "I'm not married." It was a man's condition to feel guilty. I went back to sleep trying not to let the guilt bother me.

When I awoke the sun had just cleared the horizon and the heat radiating through the window felt good on my face. During the night the bus had gone away from the mountains and we were rolling through the flat land of western Kansas. Off on the horizon I saw a tall white grain silo standing like a mute giant. Every town in this part of the country has its grain silo. Entering one town you can see the silo of the next town protruding in the air. Kansas is the beginning of the stomach of this country, the beginning of farmers and crops, grain and corn.

After a stop for breatfast in a small town cafe filled with men talking about the weather and how good the crops were doing, we piled back on the bus. There were six of us on the bus now. One black man sitting in front, two kids probably going to see relatives in Kansas City, three Mexicans who must have been wetbacks trying to get anywhere, and myself. None of us talked or acknowledged each other in any way. It didn't matter. It was Kansas.

Filled with pancakes, I was suddenly lonely. The bus was alien, the people were strangers. The land going by outside the window could have been Russia, China, France or Mexico. It didn't matter. I didn't know anybody for hundreds and hundreds of miles. If I died then nobody would know me. They would just stand around me and say. "Look at that. That young man just sat there looking out the window and died. I wonder who in the hell he is." I thought back on the night with Terry. The feel of her skin against my body. The smoothness of her inner thigh and the rise and fall of her ribs into my sides. It was good and it was fun in its own way but at that moment I felt empty and used. What was making love without love? There was no peace in my heart, no glow in my mind, no soft caring touches lingering on my skin. I wished I could fly. I would have leaped from the bus and soared up into the sky to ride with the wind currents back to LA. Love would have carried me. Storms and lightning and wind would not hurt me, knowing love was my protector. I would have flown to Barbara's and she would be sunning on the beach. I would land at her feet and give her a cloud for a present. Then I would have told her how much I missed her and she would laugh, smile, and reach out and touch my lips with her fingers and the feel of love would rush through my veins.

I sat and wallowed in my loneliness, oblivious to the bus or the land. Millions of wheat stalks saw me go by without my acknowledging their existence. The bus lurched to a stop and the driver hollered, "Tribune! Lunch stop, be here about an hour." He was swallowed into the cafe. I shook my head, knowing I had lost a few hours that I would never regain. Outside the bus the black man was smoking a cigarette and turned away when I stepped off the bus. The three Mexicans stayed on the bus, no doubt afraid they would be caught. Inside the cafe three men sat in a far booth drinking coffee and they nodded at me when I looked at them as I was headed for a table. I was not hungry and ordered coffee. I no longer felt sorry for myself. I didn't feel much of anything.

All bus stops seem to have one thing in common. They look tired and they seem to be filled with lost dreams. The walls, whether freshly painted or drab and dirty, are filled with dead dreams never realized. Through the window of the cafe I could see the face of one of the Mexicans. I knew he was hungry and so were his friends. I motioned to him but he turned his face quickly. One learns not to trust many people in life. The friendly ones can hurt you. Ironic, when one lets himself open, he can be hurt. Enemies do not hurt you, only one's friends. The black man walked back and forth in front of the window not looking in. From his face and the faces of the three men at the other booth. I could see they hated each other in about equal parts.

The coffee was strong. Too strong. Strong and bitter like the men at the booth. I felt like hell and wished I was back on the bus and we were going past Kansas countryside and I could return to my dream of Barbara.

I took another sip of coffee and put two quarters on the table. Walking out I bought three doughnuts from under the plastic display and once on the bus gave one to each of the Mexicans. They seemed surprised and looked at me with cold hard eyes. I walked away quickly and went to my seat not wanting to make them feel they had to thank me.

It seemed like hours before the bus driver got back into his seat and the bus lurched back on the highway. For some reason I did not like that little town with its men sitting in the coffee shop. I didn't like the doughnuts under plastic or the coffee that was too black and too strong. I didn't like the sight of the wheat going by or the circling crows. One of the Mexicans walked back to me and held out a gin bottle. The Beefeaters label looked like a halo. I smiled faintly and took a large swallow and handed the bottle back to him. He nodded his head, his eyes not once softening. I nodded back and felt the burn of the gin from my lips to the pit of my stomach. If I had been in a bar maybe I would have just gone up and slammed somebody in the side of the head. I shut my eyes and tired to picture Barbara's eyes and her small delicate smile. "I need, I need," rambled through my mind. "I need," and then sleep came to me with the day and the wheat fields and the rolling of the bus.

Some people say dreams are an extension of oneself. That inside of your mind are millions of universes untouched. And these tiny universes come to us in dreams, expressing our wants and needs. Taking care of things inside us that we do not even know we need. If this is so then most of the time I would just as soon not dream. I would much rather sleep and know only of darkness and wake to find another day without the torment of dreams. With dreams, sleep knows no rest, with dreams, loneliness is personified.

I awoke from the dream nervous, wanting to reach out for Barbara or Terry or others before them. The dream alive in my mind had not dissipated with consciousness. There was a soldier when I first got to the war. It was my first night on bunker duty and I was afraid. The bunkers circled our camp like large portions of castles housing machine guns and rats. The insides smelled like pee and fear but one stayed in them when it was dark, peering out past the barbed wire into the jungle that crawled with the enemy. When I walked down to the bunker for the first time during the last rays of sunlight, the soldier was sitting on the top of the bunker smoking a cigarette. "You shouldn't sit there," I spoke. He looked at me and laughed but said nothing. When it grew dark he stayed on top of the bunker smoking another cigarette and then climbed down and came into the bunker. We sat beside one another peering through the small opening of the sand bags looking for movement of any kind and not talking. We were so close to one another that we could hear each other breathe and smell the sweat of each other's body. After a while he mumbled, "They're all lying assholes, every last fucking one of them."

"Who?" I asked.

"Governments. Every one of them," he answered. At the time I was filled with pride and valor and freedom and felt I was a savior to the world. An American. Better than the rest. God chosen. Destined. He continued. "They all sit in their ivory towers and tell us what we need and want. No taxes. Freedom. Long life. Jobs. But they all want the same. Control and power."

"Not America," I retorted. He laughed and we did not talk the rest of the night. Six months later I would sit on the top of the bunker and smoke and look out into the lush jungle and I knew I felt like the man I had met earlier during the year. I felt old, lifeless and tired. Disillusioned by all forms of government and control. And although I knew there was no direction in my feelings, no answer to the world's problems, I also knew I no longer cared if there were answers or not. There was only life and death. Freedom and justice and valor and pride and whether one was an American or a German or a Jew or a Russian didn't really make much difference when it all got down to the bottom line. They were all liars.

In the dream I saw the man sitting on the bunker. He was sitting and smiling and there was a clean bullet hole between his eyes but he was still alive. As the dream ended he laughed. "See they even lied about death. There is no death. It's all just one long living nightmare. Life leads to more life, on and on forever.

Looking around the bus I saw the Mexicans were asleep. The gin must have been gone. The black man was reading a newspaper. The back of the bus driver's head radiated the feeling of boredom.

Governments regulate what one becomes: bus driver, banker, soldier, mechanic. Every job makes one a living but it enables the machine to keep going and expanding. If man worked for man there would be no government, just the benefit of man to work for. I remember a speech on television a while back. The made-up and smiling president looked at all his constituents and went on and on about the need for space travel and the need for jets to go faster and faster and the need for defense and more jobs. I wonder what the government would come up with if one day all the workers of the world got together and started tearing down all the things the governments stated we needed. Tore down all the missile silos and the bombers, tore down the factories and insurance companies, tore down the capitals and the police academices and said what we need is the world. Not governments but the world. What we need is food and medicine and love. Not factories and pullution and being told what we need. We know what we need. Food and medicine and love. I wonder what the politicans would do. They wouldn't have a job paid for by us. They wouldn't have fancy cars or paid vacations or gold credit cards. They couldn't assign contracts or billions of dollars or sit around and discuss what all the people who cannot think for themselves need. I would like to see that one day. Life for the people and of the people. I wonder how many docotrs there would be in the world if they didn't make more money than the majority of us. Would they heal and cure for the sake of humanity or the sake of belonging to the country club or the tennis club or the vacation each year?

The bus hit a bump in the road and my mind came back to the real world. Nothing would change. The rich would be rich and the governments would be governments and we would fight and continue to fight. And the poor would starve and stay uneducated while other people would spend thousands on vacations and fancy cars and big houses. I wonder if in the future one day all the children of the nations will get up in the morning and say, "This is wrong, I am a product of the world. It is the world that matters. Not the boundry we make into this country."

I looked at the sleeping Mexicans. Running from a country where there was nothing for them. But this country would offer them nothing but shacks to live in and minimum wage and lousy food and lousy health care because they did not have Blue Cross and Blue Shield for $2,200.00 a year. What did they give a fuck? A bottle of gin, a good meal and that was life. Stupidity or ignorance was an answer for power. Educate only the rich and you might maintain your power. Put education costs so hight that the poor must remain poor and be laborers and you have a chance for power. An educated man would not work at a factory or shovel coal or pump gas or vacuum your office building.

Kansas was changing. Gone were the flat plains covered with wheat and dotted with small towns and their towering grain silos. Now the country rolled from hill to hill and was covered with trees and houses. The rural road became a four lane freeway as we neared Kansas City and the occasional traffic became a steady stream of automobiles. It was not too far into the past that wagon trains started out from there headed for Santa Fe and points west and south. The three Mexicans were awake, each peering out of a window. On the horizon I could see a green cloud marking the edge of the city. It's politicans or industry that own politicans who keep the factories belching gas that one day will kill us all under the name of progress and jobs. Maybe we need jobs but we need the right jobs. That is the difference between politicans and humanity. Humanity needs jobs that do not destroy our planet. Politicans need listeners. I needed a lobotomy.

Entering Kansas City I thought of driving into LA with Barbara and ignoring the green cloud that surrounded us. There was only her smile and my thoughts of her. Now there was only that bus and a black man and three Mexicans and the green cloud that was much like the inside of a fortune teller's ball knowing the future.

In Kansas City, Kansas, I changed buses and was on my way in only a few minutes. The bus was filled with many people. Mostly blacks. With old clothes and old shoes talking in whispers among themselves because there were a few white people on the bus. We drove over the bridge to Kansas City, Missouri, and the bus headed north towards Iowa. Maybe in Iowa there was the dream I sought. The thought that would send me off into the world with a heart and hopes and dreams, not bitter and angry. I wondered what the people on the bus thought when they saw me look them over and try to understand what had put us on that bus together. I wondered if there was anybody who truly hoped in this modern world or if only the people on television commercials smiled and felt secure.

Outside of Kansas City we finally left the green haze of progress and modernization. The air that led us into the future. The country was cornfields and small wooden houses painted white with wraparound porches. Horses lazed with Jersey and Holstein cows and tomatoes started to burst forth from garden plots. I began to see and remember portions of life when there were dreams and hopes, and love was taken for granted. It was a strange feeling that entered my mind. A feeling of age and the knowledge of time.

I wished Barbara was there. I wished I could hold her hand and point out trees and cows and white frame houses. I wished we could wave at a man on a tractor. I would tell her that was when I had heart. That was when America was proud and strong and did not lie or sell out to the oil companies. That was before I knew the automobile was killing us or that people lied. I wished she could see the crows circling over the cornfields or the small ponds we passed filled with bass and catfish and blue gill. I wondered if she had received my letter and if she had, had she just smiled and toss- ed it in the garbage, passing our days off as nice but not anything that had not faded by then. I wondered if all love fades or if we just grow accustomed to being alone.

When I was a small boy, my grandmother and I were fishing a pond that was on their farm. The fish were not biting and we were not talking. I was watching a big green bullfrog eye a dragonfly when my grandmother sighed and murmured, "Love lies bleeding." I looked at her and her eyes were far off beyond the hill to the south, beyond the earth or the heavens. I did not say anything but that night, laying in my bed listening to the chorus of crickets and the bullfrogs; I thought about her words, love lies bleeding. The words did not make any sense and I filed them somewhere in my little boy mind. They popped out years later and I realized that even my grandmother had been sad during her life. And I was sad because when I was a boy I could not hold her and say, "I understand, It's okay. I understand and I love you."

The bus made its way through individual small towns, all of them the same with a town square where the courthouse was; a tractor sales, a car shop, several small restaurants and a series of small wooden houses with bird baths and flowers blooming in the yards. The women were big women. The men strong. Corn-fed midwest people. White people with roots back to Europe. Farmers. Here was part of the world where it was good to have been a soldier. Good to believe in America. Here the propaganda and lies could stand up and the flag still flew in many yards. Here the churches were filled on Sunday and old women and men sang hymns and visited cemeteries where relatives were buried. It was a changing world though. Still clinging to old values but changing. A world eaten up now by factories and foreign trade and embargos. Eaten up by politicans in big cities who did not know where their food came from except when it was served by waiters in red coats and smiling faces; or, explained by do-good actors playing roles and making a few bucks before heading back to LA. I looked at the passing people and had to smile. It was good to believe, even if the belief was shrouded in lies.

We passed a sign saying simply: WELCOME TO IOWA. Nobody on the bus seemed to notice. I felt I was entering the land of OZ. Off to find a dream, off to find a ghost I left somewhere in that breadbasket of American life. Somewhere with the corn and tomatoes and slow-moving, hardworking people there was a thread that would begin to weave for me once again a reason for life and government and wonder.

During jungle training I met a man from Iowa. A boy, I suppose. I was a boy and thought I was a man. He was a true farm boy. Chewed tobacco, smiled all the time. When we would get passes and go into town, he would spend all his money on the whores. He did it because in Iowa on the farm there was nothing like it. It was all fun and games. He did not see the misery. He truly thought the whores liked it. I called him Home. Not like the blacks who called ed each other Home trying to be some sort of racial revolution. Just Home because he reminded me of a home. On our last pass before we were to head for glory he got two tattoos, one on each shoulder. One was a heart with his girl's name in it and the other was an ear of corn. He loved corn. We would sit and talk about the midwest. I had only visited my grandparents there but he was a true product of the black dirt. If you had stuck his feet in the ground in a few weeks he would have turned into a corn plant. He was killed before there was time to be disillusioned. Before there was time to read about the movies stars going to see the enemy or the fact that people hated us. I was thankful for that part of it. Since it was in the cards for him to get it, I was glad it was early. Something about dying with ideals that seemed to help. I really don't know why. I wrote his folks when it was over and told them how we used to sit and talk about the farm. He and I could sit and bring his house to us. The cackle of chickens and the mooing of the cows early in the morning. I could see this tall sister with her strong shoulders and toughened hands carrying feed to the pigs and his mother cooking breakfast. I never received an answer from them nor did I expect one. It just seemed like a good thing to do at the time. If I was in a war now I don't know if I would do it. I don't know if I would want strangers in on my family's deaths or hear from someone who had seen my son killed.

The bus left the freeway and a few miles down a narrow winding road it stopped in front of another cafe. This was it. After all the miles I had come to the town looking for the beginning. I was the only one to leave the bus and as it pulled away I looked at the tall silver water tower in the center of town and down the street at the newspaper office and several now abandoned stores. None of my relatives remained there. They were all in the cemetery on the edge of town. But I could see myself as a child walking down the street with my grandmother going to the drugstore with its old counter and round seats and laying a dime down for a chocolate coke.

CHAPTER VIII

The town was like all the other little towns of southern Iowa. The courthouse sat in the middle of town with a road that completely circled it and roads led off of this road lined with wooden houses. There was a line of old men sitting on the benches around the courthouse. The men had on white socks and overalls and each wore a hat of different size, color and shape. One could spend a few days with them and learn the history of the area for generations back — in between checkers and spitting tobacco and farting. Around the courthouse on the opposite side the street were various stores. Most were vacant. But there still was a grocery store, a hardware store and to my surprise a video rental. The old barber shop was gone but peering into the window I could see the chair covered with dust. An antique collector will pick it up one day for a song and sell it in New York or LA. I noticed the eyes of the old men following me as I walked around the courthouse. They were trying to figure out who I was. Strangers did not stop in small towns just to look at old abandoned stores. And the people of these little towns were suspicious of strangers. I decided to walk over and say hello, tell them who I was.

As I neared the line of six old men, their faces began to take on names but I couldn't remember the names. Each of the men I had met with my grandparents. I was a few steps away when the old man on the end of the bench smiled at me and stood up. "Frank," he spoke holding out his hand. "You're Frank, Billie and Bob's boy. Ruth's grandson. We thought that was you. Could tell by your walk. You walk like your father did when he was a boy." I shook his hand and he sat down. One at a time the men stood and shook my hand. They had firm handshakes and even time had not removed the callouses from their hands. One of the men was George, had a farm by my grandparent's. One was Clyde. Used to drive the school bus and work for all of them. One was Oscar. He was the repair man for the hardware store. Pyfer used to own a grocery store. Looking at them I felt old and they seemed like children.

"What brings you back to Iowa?" one of these children asked.

I leaned up against the trunk of the oak tree by the bench. "Just came back to take a look."

"Town's changed a lot, Frank," Pyfer spoke, not sadly, not bitterly. Just the facts. "Farms going under. Stores going under. Nothing left but old people now. Town's dying. Young have gone off to the big cities to make a living. Come back like you do every so often to try and remember." He spit a blob of tobacco on the grass. "How's your folks?"

"Folks are fine."

One of the men laughed. "Your father was a pistol, let me tell you. That son of a bitch was always in some kind of trouble." The men all laughed. I smiled. My eyes caught the front of the old movie theater across the road. It was boarded up. Movies used to be a dime, popcorn a dime. I did not miss the past but it was hard to fully realize how fast the time had gone by. When I was twelve I came back for the summer and I met a girl who was my third or fourth cousin removed. She lived several blocks from my grandmother and I would go over every day. She had blue eyes and blonde hair and was slim like I am. We played down by the river and talked. I told her about the city. In the middle of the summer we started holding hands and then made ourselves a small hiding place in the back of the large and dense stand of trees. We took a blanket and a pillow there and had a stash of candy bars and soda pop. Sitting in our hiding place one afternoon we suddenly kissed. Not a tongue probing kiss of passion but with just our lips. Walking back from our secret spot I was in love. I left her on the porch of her house and going back to my grandmother's was like walking off to war to never return. The night went on forever as I tossed and turned thinking about the girl and the kiss. The next night we went to the movies. I treated, buying popcorn and sodas. We sat and watched the movie and held hands. All during the movie I wanted to reach out and grab her breast. I wanted to run my hand up her dress. I was so filled with lust I thought I would die or the pounding of my heart could be heard echoing off the walls by everybody in the theater. After the movie while I was walking her home we stopped by the garbage cans of the darkened house and kissed again. Only that time our tongues flicked out and touched each other's. My hand ran up her side to her breasts and we were both on fire. But we stopped and then ran to our respective homes. For the whole summer we kissed and petted and panted and talked about getting married when we were eighteen. We went to movies and held hands and she sat and watched me when I played Little League ball. I picked flowers for her and we stole watermelons and when the summer was over and I was on the bus back to Texas I thought I would die. We wrote every day for a month or so and then we no longer wrote. The next summer I saw her but she had another boy friend. I was in the army when she was married. She wrote my mother and told her to tell me. I heard a few years ago that she had three kids and they all lived in Seattle where her husband sells insurance. Funny. When I was in Seattle I didn't think about her. Looking at the movie house I could feel the small rise of her breast and the pink tip of her young tongue darting across my lips.

"Where are you going to stay, Frank?" one of the old men asked.

"Anybody renting rooms in town?"

"Remember Grace? She used to help your grandmother put up tomatoes?" I nodded my head. "Well, she's renting rooms. Go down Third Street over there a block and it's the two story white house on the corner. She'll remember you."

Feeling out of place, I nodded to the old men and walked off.

Leaving the square I passed the wooden frame homes with the large wraparound porches. The day was hot and sticky and my hand on the handle of the suitcase was sweating. Knocking on the door of the house I heard the slow movement coming to the door. The old woman was hunched over at the shoulders. She wore a flower print dress and her snow white hair was in a tight bun. On her feet were black round toed shoes that laced. The flesh on her arms hung down and moved as she stood looking at me. Her eyes were alive and piercing. "Well, Frank," she spoke in a moment. "How have you been?' The years melted away and seemed like a mere day. "Come in, come in." She opened the door. Inside was dark and cool, smelling of age and dust. I followed her into the kitchen with its linoleum floor and metal kitchen table by the window. "I was just about to eat a bite. Join me." I sat down and she moved slowly around the kitchen. She put out bread and butter, a dish of onions and cucumbers in vinegar and sugar. Out of the refrigerator cold chicken and bean salad. Sitting down she said a prayer and I bowed my head. "You look good, Frank," she spoke between small bites of chicken. "Last time I saw you was at the funeral. Not many of us old people left now. I'm one of the last." I smiled "Tomatoes are good this year. A lot of people around town have already come to me to put up their tomatoes." She pointed to the cupboard. "Still have beans and tomatoes from last year. Before you leave town let me give you some."

"I hear you are renting rooms," I stated simply.

She looked at me. "I'm renting George's room." There was no sadness in her voice speaking her dead husband's name. "Five dollars a day."

"I would like to stay here for a week."

"Sure Frank, I would be happy to have you." with lunch finished I started to clean off my place and put the dishes in the sink. "You just leave them there." She led me to the stairs. "I don't go up there anymore but the room is up and to the right. The bath is at the top of the stairs."

I went up the stairs and each one creaked as I stepped on it. The room was musty. There was four-poster bed, a chair with a large mirror against the wall and a closet. The light was in the middle of the ceiling and went on and off with a string that hung down. Two windows with faded white curtains were on two of the four walls. I opened the windows and put the sticks under them to keep them open. Both windows faced into large maple trees. It was an old house with an old woman and the windows faced old trees. I felt calm, for a moment time was not passing. It was constant and there was no change, only now, forever.

When I left the room and walked down the stairs and out of the house, Grace was in the yard bending over picking dandelions. She did not see me and instead of bothering her I walked by. I wanted to go see my grandparent's house and see what time had done.

I had two sets of grandparents who lived in that small town. Ruth and Bill, my mother's parents, lived in town. Audry and Olon, my father's parents, lived on a small farm outside of town a few miles. Both of the men had been in the navy during the war and when I was young they would talk of war at times when they were filled with a few beers or a couple of shots of whiskey when my mother or grandmother was not around. It was not brave talk or talk of killing but it was talk of the oneness of the men and the feelings of war. When both of my grandfathers were dead, for some reason each of my grandmothers during different visits showed me pictures of them as young men in uniform. They stood tall and straight with groups of their friends. One picture showed Grandfather Bill with his friends holding a captured Japanese flag. Both of my grandparents hated the Japanese and hated the idea of foreigners being allowed in this country. I did not understand the hate but I was well-versed in love of country. When I joined the army I received letters from my grandmothers but they were not filled with the honor and the gusty words of my grandfathers when they were alive. Men fight. Women stay home. Both in their own way at war.

I was walking along a cracked and ancient sidewalk. Grass grew between the cracks. That sidewalk had seen the feet of my parents and their parents and their parents before them. In the limbs of the large oak trees squirrels darted and large jay birds scolded their business. Most of the houses I passed were vacant and the windows boarded up. It was like the old men had told me, the town was dying. When I was young nothing died but now even towns die. I walked around the corner looking intently at the cracks of the sidewalk and lifted my head to look at the two story house where my grandparents lived. But it was gone. The lot between two other houses was empty except for a scraped patch of bare dirt. Everything left my mind. There was no sidewalk, no trees, no grass, no remembrance of prison or war. Nothing. Reeling in a void I leaned up against the nearest tree and looked at the bare dirt. I shut my eyes and pictured the old house. The front yard was small, not more than twenty yards of grass and a walk led to the front porch. On the porch there was a wooden swing and three metal rocking chairs, each with its own individual cushion. The front door led into a room and to its right was the living room. Off of the main room was the kitchen. The windows were thick bevel ed glass and in the front of the house they were framed with col- ored glass and flower boxes. There were always flowers. Azaleas and mums and in the back yard a large garden filled with corn and tomatoes and beans and a rhubarb patch for pies.

Now it was gone. No place even for the ghosts to live. No yellowed walls telling of once fresh white paint. No rooms filled with remembrances of relatives and a young boy hiding behind a chair listening to adults talking about the old days and the scandals in their lives when he should have been in bed. No smell of cigar smoke from uncles playing cards for quarters and telling dirty jokes in the kitchen. No waiting until dark to go out and hunt large night crawlers to fish the farm ponds the next day. There was nothing. Nothing but the scraped black earth.

I turned from the emptiness and walked quickly away. I could see the ghosts of my grandparents floating above the ground, tears in their eyes. No rest, there was no rest. Grace was still in the front yard but she saw me and stopped searching for dandelions. "I wanted to tell you, Frank," she said "But I couldn't find the way." I nodded my head and walked into the house and up to my room. It was cool and the lace curtains moved gently in the breeze. I stood by the window and looked into the deep green leaves of the tree. Tears formed in the corners of my eyes and I let them run down my face. God, there was nobody to touch. Nobody to rest my head upon. Nobody to turn to and smile faintly and feel their comfort in my heart.

I had no idea how long I stood there by the window. It was dark when I was conscious of Grace's call from downstairs. "Frank? Come on down. I've fixed some supper. You hear me?" I turned my leaden feet from the window, wiped my face and left the room. "Coming," I answered, going into the bathroom. I washed my face and took several deep breaths.

Grace was sitting at the table. She had fried pork chops and gravy and there were green beans steaming in a pot and several large red tomatoes. "Tomatoes are a little green," she stated. "But they will do." I sat down and looked at her old strong face and smiled faintly. I took two pork chops and tore up several pieces of bread, poured gravy over them and then cut up a tomato. We ate in silence for a few moments. "I was born outside this town like your grandmother was, Frank," Grace stated like she was reading a history book. "Your grandmother and I were born about fifty acres apart. Several days apart. In those days it was a lot different. We worked. We all worked. There was no machinery. Only horses and hands. Ruth and I went to the same little schoolhouse out in the country. There was fifteen of us kids, ranging in age from six to seventeen. The schoolhouse was one room with a big potbellied stove in it and unless the snow was over your head, you went to school. All the people are gone now. Both farms have been sold. The schoolhouse is gone. But you know, Frank? I can lay down on my bed at night and I can see the houses and the school and the people just like they were alive and right here before us. Life is nothing but dreams, Frank. Dreams don't die or grow old or get pushed aside by progress. They stay if you let them. They stay forever, until somebody holds you as a dream."

"But it's sad, Grace," I answered.

Grace smiled and shook her head. "No. No, it's not sad, It's life, child. Life and only life. It's only sad if you make it." We finished eating and she got up to shuffle to the refrigerator and took out a bowl of Jello. "My husband loved this stuff," she laughed sitting back down. "When we were first married we lived on a small farm. Didn't have a refrigerator or anything like that. We had a cave on the place where we kept things we wanted to stay cool. When we moved into town and had electricity and a refrigerator, the first time I made Jello you should have seen his eyes light up. It was like magic." She spooned a large spoonful of orange Jello into a bowl for me and set it down. "Change is all you can ever count on, Frank. Take it from an old lady. Change is all you can ever count on."

I ate the Jello and felt good inside, thinking of the man who loved it so. "You can count on how you feel about somebody. You know this." She reached over with her old withered hand and touched my face and sighed. Over her protests I cleared the table and put the dishes in the sink and poured us two cups of coffee from the steaming pot on the stove. "You sit and drink your coffee and I'll do the dishes." She sipped her coffee and watched. When I finished I sat down.

With the coffee finished, I followed her outside and we sat on the porch. She had two high-backed wooden rocking chairs. Across the street several fireflies danced between the bushes and I could hear people laughing down the block. "It's hard to believe I've been in this area eighty-seven years, Frank. I can sit here at night alone when it's nice and remember being young and in love. I can remember kissing my first boy not far from here on a night my father let us come into town. I can remember making love for the first time, like it was yesterday. I can remember each of my children being born and I can remember three of them dying. I have had a long good life." She fell silent and only the creak of the two rocking chairs filled the night. There were more fireflies across the yard. They danced and darted, looking like many tinkerbells. I looked at the old lady and then down the street into the darkness to the empty lot where my grandparent's house used to stand and I made a wish. Tinkerbell lived somewhere. She would never change.

The house was dark and silent. The two rocking chairs rested on the front porch, empty. Grace slept in her bed and I sat in a chair in front of the open window looking from the dark into the dark. A chorus of crickets filled the night and in between the shadows of three branches I could see a few stars shining. My grandmother used to tell me stars are symbols of hope. Whenever I was sad in my life I could always look at the stars. During the war at night it was easy to let fear take hold of one's thoughts. Sitting poised like some demon waiting to split the darkness with bullets, I would always think about the stars and how the unseen enemy saw the same stars as I. It was an eerie thought. Both of us blanketed by the same sights. And I would wonder if he was afraid too and if the men I killed or the man who would kill me saw and felt the same thing before the moment of truth. Most people I have met in my older years do not look at the stars. They see the stars on television or the stars at a movie but they do not look at the stars in the night sky. There are too many lights in town to see them. Governments spend billions of dollars to explore the heavens but most of us here on earth do not see the night stars. It is as though we are afraid to look up at night. Afraid or ashamed before something that has seen us from the beginning. I thought about the first night with Barbara. With her lying on the blanket beside me and I not thinking about her firm breast or wondering about her thighs as she slept. But instead thinking about the stars and how they covered us and how fate had brought us to the same point in time to share a blanket on the desert floor of Arizona. I wonder if, before she fell asleep, she wondered if I would make a pass at her. Tell her some old phrase of courtship like "You have pretty eyes," or "I feel like I have known you before." I wish I could have brought Barbara here. Here years ago when the vacant lot still was home to the demolished house. Here to sit on the porch with my relatives and talk about old things and old times and say hello to darkened forms walking by as we rocked in the rocking chairs and talked. I stood up from the chair and made my way out of the dark house closing the door quietly behind me. In this town one did not have to worry about being mugged at night and I walked slowly towards the square and the lone pay phone in front the old Texaco gas station. I stood by the phone ignoring the swarm of small beetles and moths attracted to the dim light. A truck passed by, a boy and a girl sitting next to each other. I dialed O and gave the operator Barbara's number. "Collect," I said. "Collect from Frank." As the number rang I felt nervous and could hear my heart pounding in my chest. The phone rang six or seven times and I was about to hang up when Barbara answered. The operator's voice said, "Collect from Frank." There was a slight pause and then Barbara answered, "Yes."

"Hello kid."

Barbara's voice was soft and low. "Hello Frank. I received your letter." I had forgotten that I wrote. "Where are you?"

"I'm in Iowa." There was a pause. "I miss you, Barbara," I spoke trying to fill my words with my feelings.

"Are you okay, Frank?" she asked sounding concerned.

"I'm okay. A little tired but okay."

"Good." She sounded relieved. "I miss you too, Frank, Strange, huh cowboy?"

I laughed. "Sure is." The dam broke. "God, Barbara, I wish I was with you. Just sitting in a room with you, watching television, anything. Just with you."

"You know where I live. I'm here," she commented. I wanted to tell her I had slept with a lady I met at the bus station. I wanted to tell her about my grandparent's house being gone. I wanted to tell her I would like to take a shower with her and feel the warmth of her towels and the smell of her perfume in the air. I wanted to tell her that I dreamed about her. We were both quiet then she broke the silence. "Are you coming back, Frank?"

I looked up at the stars. A few bugs were hittng me on the face. "I think so, Barbara."

Barbara took a deep breath. "I'm here, Frank. Remember that, I'm here. Okay?"

"Okay," I answered.

"Bye."

"Bye," I responded and we hung up. I walked back to the house slowly. I wondered why we needed anybody. Why, in this dog eat dog world, in the cold and the darkness, we had to let our defenses down and need somebody. Why was it so important to pick up the phone and stammer and feel awkard just to let somebody know you are alive and that you need and feel.

I sat in one of the rockers on the porch. I had not seen any of the men I was in the army with since the war. They were men I became closer to than my brother. Men I cried with and cussed with and hated with. Men I changed with and became disillusioned with. I wondered if they were like me. Sitting somewhere alone, lost in many ways. Wanting to reach out and tell somebody to hold them but afraid of the feeling. The vulnerability of being close to somebody. The risk of trusting or crying with joy of knowing warmth. No longer believing in governments or causes. No longer believing in anything. I remembered the last look at many of the men I knew. We shook hands and turned our backs on each other and went our own ways. Taking a part of each of us with one another. Not looking back but never really looking forward. Our faces were like the faces of many of the convicts I had met. Faces stuck in time. Knowing time as most people never know time. Day to day, minute to minute, second to second. Passing, passing to nothing but time. No hope, no dream, no Christmas, no Easter, no Thanksgiving, no Happy Birthday. Just time. Time, on and on until no time. Time when one could not think or would not have to suppress dreams and hopes would no longer need anything.

The truck with the two lovers passed by the house. Two lovers that wished the night would stay forever. That all they would ever know was the touch of each other and the sound of the engine and the feeling of their hearts as they drove around that small midwestern Iowa town that was dying. I got up from the porch and started to walk once again. The old highway ran north out of town past the fairgrounds where once a year in August all the farmers in the area came to show off pigs and chickens, cows and horses. Eat pies and cakes, judge jellies and jams, and be with others of their kind. Off of that old highway ran gravel roads leading to the scattered farmhouses. The old farm was not more than five or six miles outside of town. I walked beside the highway. Past the dark buildings of the fairground. Past lights in the distance that were the outside lights in front of farmhouses. By then Barbara was asleep. Maybe she was wrapped in the arms of another lover. How could I have expected her to wait? Wait for what? A man she met beside the highway? But I longed for her. I wanted to feel her nipples against my lips and the touch of her fingers running through my hair. I wanted to see the night light shadow her nakedness and have her pelvis rise to me as I entered her. I walked alone with the chorus of frogs in the ditch water beside the highway, dreaming of a lady that something inside of me kept me from returning to.

The horizon was purple and the miles of cornfields seemed like mute people when a tractor chugged by me going in the opposite direction. The farmer waved but did not slow down. Walking by a farmhouse I could see a woman in a kitchen and hear the beginning cackles of the chickens waiting to be let out of the hen house. There was the smell of ancient things in the air as I walked by the awakening farm. Not like the beginning of day in a city with the cussing and spurting cars. The hurried showers and planning of meetings for the day. But I knew even there the farm had its pressures. But I was an observer and could hold onto the feeling of peace and solitude that surrounded me. The sun was barely above the horizon when I was standing by my grandparent's old farm. The barn that seemed so large when I was young was just a fallen in small red building. The feedlot was overgown with weeds and the door was hanging lopsided by one rusted hinge. The chicken house was fallen in too and the house had been taken apart. Doors and windows were missing. I walked inside the house and looked at the animal-fouled linoleum floor of the kitchen and remembered the sound of the women as they cooked large Sunday dinners while the men sat at the pond fishing and talking about the weather. I remembered the dogs sitting patiently in the yard waiting for the leftovers and the cats that kept to the safety of the wooden fence, biding their time to spring for a small piece of chicken from the dogs. Leaving the house I thought maybe it would have been better if that house was like the house in town. Gone, completely dismantled, so only the dream remained, not the mark of time. I left the house and walked out to the pond, the pond where I caught my first fish. A few fish dimpled the surface and I smiled. A muskrat swam leisurely for his burrow. If my grandfather had been alive the muskrat would have been dodging a blast from a shotgun. Out in the fields crows bounced around picking grasshoppers warming in the sun. There were no ghosts there, only memories. Walking back towards town on the gravel road a dusty Ford pickup stopped and a man my age rolled down the window. "Need a ride?" he asked. I looked at his sunburned face and the dirty cap on his head. "I'm going to town. Hop in." I got in the truck. "I seen you this morning walking through the old place. I own it now. Bought it a few years back." We drove by a neat farmhouse with a new barn. "That's my place." The place looked alive and fresh. "When me and the wife have kids, I'm going to give them the old place. Fix it up and let them live there." We did not talk the rest of the way into town. He let me out a block from Grace's house. "Thanks," I muttered and waved as he drove off.

Grace was out in the yard attacking the dandelions again. "Damn dandelions," she proclaimed. "Get them out and they all come back. It's an endless battle." I walked inside the house and went up and packed my bag. Back outside I walked up to Grace and kissed her on the forehead. "You look like your father, Frank," she said. I smiled faintly and headed for the bus stop. The old men were already congregating at the court house and I waved from across the street. Sitting in the cafe where the bus would stop I sipped on a cup of coffee and listened to WHO radio out of Des Moines. The stock prices were on and several farmers listened intently. In my pocket was a bus ticket for Huntsville, Texas. I wanted to go back and look at the prison from the outside. I didn't know what is was in me that pulled me to do that. But it was there. There like my grandparent's house that was gone.

I did not look at the town as the bus pulled away. I tried to remember the dream. The dream when I was young and all the houses were freshly painted and the flowers bloomed and all the old people were my age. Together and in love.

It was dark and the man sitting next to me slept soundly. When he got on the bus in Missouri and sat down we had said hello and that had been the extent of our conversation. All during the day and into the night I had tried to think of nothing but thoughts jumped in and out of my mind with no order or reason. I wished I had gone to the cemetery back in Iowa and had seen my relatives but I did not. I could see a time when even the cemetery would be overgrown with weeds and the markers unreadable. I thought about Grace when she was young with a girlish figure and not old with sagging breasts and pale wrinkled skin. I thought about the farmers hanging onto old dreams about farms and pigs and chickens and going under, not letting go of their stubborn beliefs. I thought the government or big business or whoever ran the government had a conspiracy going to wipe out the farms and middle America in time. Then we would only have the rich and the poor. The slave owners and the slaves. Strange but if you're not rich you're a slave. White, black, yellow, red. It makes no difference. If you're not rich you work for minimum wage and eagerly gobble up the miniscule treats the rich hand out for a job well done. A week vacation once a year. A one-hundred dollar bonus for Christmas. People laud the system. Both parents working to make ends meet but nothing changes. The rich pay no taxes and the middle pays for everything.

The bus stopped in another small town and the man next to me rose and got off. We were there for no more than fifteen minutes and then once again were on the road.

The bus was moving before I noticed a man in uniform walking down the aisle. He stopped by the vacant seat next to me and took off his cap. "Sir, is this seat taken?"

"No, sit down," I answered. He sat down after putting his hat on the overhead rack. Looking at him I smiled. His face was clean, barely shaving I guessed. His hair gone. The shirt collar sticking above the green army coat was heavily pressed. The stripe of PFC was on his shoulder. In his lap had a brown envelope carrying his orders for his duty assignment. "Going back off leave?" I asked. I remembered taking the bus from Louisiana to Austin after basic to see my girlfriend who was in college. And having to get back on the bus and head for California after spending a week with her. During that week it was the first time I had ever slept with a girl I loved. We rented a room in a small shabby motel on the edge of Austin and drank wine and fell clumsily into each other's arms. Leaving Austin, my heart felt as though it would fall into my stomach. The private looked at me and I could see the sadness in his young eyes. "Yes, sir," he answered. "Going to Louisiana for advanced infantry training."

"I did my basic there."

He looked at me with an inquisitive look. Hoping I could help him and take some of the butterflies out of his stomach. "How was it?' he asked.

"Asshole of the country," I commentd dryly. "Next to 'Nam it has to be the lousiest place I have ever seen in my life." The private smiled. "That's what I heard."

"But," I continued, "it all passes. Just tell yourself that. Each day is one less day you have to spend in training."

"You go to 'Nam?" the boy asked. I nodded my head. "How was it?"

I shrugged my shoulders. "Nothing much to speak about. Hopefully you won't have to find out."

I looked at the boy. There was nothing to say. Nothing to tell him about war and pain, death. Nothing about valor or glory or any of the high ideals believed in then. "I was your age when I went. I suppose I would do the same thing again."

"You guys sure got fucked around," he added.

"Guess so," I answered. "Got a girl?" I spoke changing the subject.

He nodded his head and reached into his back pocket and pulled out his billfold. In the dim light I looked at the photograph of a young smiling girl posing by an old Chevy pick up. She had on short pants and a tight blouse and her shoulders were held back giving a good view of her breasts. "Lovely, She is lovely."

He put the billfold back into his pocket. "I'll marry her when I get out. She already said yes."

I thought back to Jan. Lovely Jan with the big tits and the big smile. Jan the lady I wrote everyday from 'Nam. Jan, who I wrote poems and bled my heart to. Jan, whose picture I carried in my helmet. Jan who I dreamed of kissing and stroking. Jan the girl who wrote me and told me it was hard to go to college and think about somebody in Vietnam. "I wish you both best of luck," I commented to the private.

"Guys I met in the army tell me none of the girls wait. Oh, they write for a while but then somebody else comes along and they go with them."

I looked at the boy. "You never know. Love wins at times." I did not feel confident in my words but I did not feel like telling the young soldier to forget her, time will kill it. Time and youth and distance. But I was trying to convince myself of hope so I told him you could never tell.

Jan and I were going to marry. Marry and I was going to go back to college after the army. She was going to be a teacher. I wonder where she was. "Love Lies Bleeding" entered my mind.

"You kill anybody in the war?" the soldier asked.

I looked at him and then out into the dark. It was a strange question. "Did you kill anybody?" A question that should never be asked. Like being in prison and being asked what you were in for. You just don't ask that. You might not want to know the answer. "Wars are fought to kill people." I answered and dropped the subject. He heard the agitation in my voice and looked down into his lap. "No glory in killing, son," I told him. "It's something you don't forget."

Killing. Strange, killing. All the games as a little boy, killing and dying. But then the games became real and it's no longer a game. Just death and blood and guts and the smell. I don't wake up at night thinking about the killing. I got over that. I wake up at times feeling the uselessness of it all but no longer the wonder. It makes me sick. Man wasn't born to kill or die in a war. I don't believe war was part of the master plan.

I reclined my seat back as far as possible. I did not feel tired but I shut my eyes. Gone was the soldier and the bus. If only the memories would fade away.

CHAPTER IX

In some small town the next day the soldier transferred to another bus. We did not talk much during the day although we had lunch together and laughed over similar experiences concerning basic training. When he left I wished him good luck and as I watched him walk down the aisle I wished I could go back in time and regain the beliefs he held. We were all so young and peach-faced when we landed in Vietnam. Tall and proud in our bright green fatigues. Faces filled with valor and American pride. I still had remnants of pride when I came back to the states but it did not last long. The country said the war was wrong and those of us who went were pushed to the side and ignored. Ignored in a friendly way, I suppose. People wishing we did not exist. If there were no parades or pats on the back then we would all go away and it would be okay. Life would go on in America like it should and it would all be okay.

My first day out of the army six of us took a cab to the airport to Oakland. Five men I had met at the discharge center. We had on our dress uniforms and our pockets were stuffed with mustering out pay. We sat in a small round bar after buying our tickets for different parts of the country and got drunk. Not a happy I'm-getting-drunk but just drunk. Drunk for the men still in the bunkers and going out on the ambushes. Drunk for the helicopter pilots and the door gunners. Drunk for the friends who would never get drunk again.

When my plane was called I staggered to my feet and slept until the stewardess woke me up and I was home. Home to my folks and sister and brother and a different war. A war of trying not to be different. I went fishing. I went hiking. I went to see my old girl friend and stood looking at her, wishing there was something to say but there was nothing except "Good luck" I enrolled in college but school did not seem to have the same merit. What would English and algebra and world history do for mankind? What would football games and pep rallies do for the men still fighting? It would change nothing. Every night on the news I watched the growing demonstrations against the war. I did not grow bitter, I only grew empty. I fell in with other veterans and we personified as a group the general feeling of outcasts. We started drinking and then started smoking pot. And somewhre down the road I was busted.

When the jury heard I was a veteran they scowled. I will never forget that. They scowled and figured smoking pot and being a killer was worth seven years in the pen. After endless appeals, five years later I was in prison producing for the state of Texas. There were baby killers, wife killers, rapists, bank robbers, strong armed men, and a few pot smokers.

It's a funny thing about prison but most people inside figure they should be there. Everybody inside knows about good laws and bad laws and crooked cops and good cops and judges on the take and judges that will hang you. It's part of prison. But most convicts figure out smokers are nothing. They're not even good criminals.

When I got off the bus in Huntsville, Texas, it was hot and humid. A normal east Texas town. The buildings are brick and the streets are tidy and clean. Men wore cowboy boots and hats whether they had ever been on a horse or not. The women wore neat dresses and talked with their high Texas accents. It was the south. Blacks were not equal. There was the black side of town and the white and stuck in the middle were the Mexicans.

I hailed a cab and the black driver took my bag and put it in the trunk. "Where 'ya going?" He even talked like a Texan.

"Take me out to the Wynne Unit. I want to see my old home." He looked at me but did not seem alarmed. Blacks know a lot about prison. It's no big deal. Even a felon can drive a cab. He drove through town and out on the highway he began to talk. "I takes a lot of peoples out here to visit but I's never taking one out here to look at it again."

"Just something I have to do," I answered. Out in the fields I saw convicts dressed all in white hoeing weeds between watermelons. Around them guards rode on horses with 30/30 rifles in their hands. In the distance I could see the red brick prison beginning to grow larger as we neared. At the turn off towards the visitors's parking lot I told the driver to pull off to the side of the road. I got out. A twelve foot fence surrounded the prison with the rolls of barbed wire on the top. In the four corners of the fence stood tall grey towers with guards in them. The grass around the prison was impeccable and several black convicts pruned the shrubs and bushes while another watered the yellow and red petunias. I could see the stacks from the mattress factory and trucks unloading food by the kitchen.

When they took me from here the day I was to get out, I was shackled and chained to the floor of a bus. Two hours later I was in civilian clothes and walking toward the bus with two hundred dollars in my pocket. Inside the fence were men I met who would die there. Those men did not look out of the windows. There was

no other world in their lives except the inside. A world of fluore-
cent light and television and books. To look out was to feel
something and to feel something was to want to die.

"Lots of good men in there," the cab driver stated.

"Lots of bad men too," I smiled and got back in the cab. The
driver got in and and turned around. "Where to now?"

"Take me to the airport in Houston."

"Son, that's over eighty miles."

"I don't care. Just get me to the airport."

He smiled. "Fifty bucks and I shuts off the meter."

"You got it."

He began to drive down the road and we slowly passed a column of convicts walking towards the gate. To each side of them a
guard rode with his rifle. I looked at a guard, his face pushed out
with chewing tobacco. As his eyes met mine I smiled and threw
him the finger. Several men in the column laughed. What did they
care, they were already in prison. The guard scowled and the driver
stepped on the gas.

"You see that guard's eyes?" the driver cackled. "That boy
don't even know what to think."

I felt as though I had broken a chain. A chain that circled my
heart. I didn't know why. Freedom. Maybe it was freedom.

The driver skillfully manuevered the jammed freeways of
Houston. Cussing, laughing, hogging the fancy cars, explaining,
"Fuckin' Cadillac won't hit no cab." Then we were at the airport.
I gave him sixty bucks. He smiled and got my bag. The reason a
cabby puts your bags in the trunk is if you don't pay, you don't get
your bag. Survival. Every trade has it own tricks.

As I walked through the crowded airport I felt out of place. The
airport was not a bus station. People were clean and well dressed
there. Businessmen with their Wall Street Journal and Money
magazine paraded around for the crowd. Women clicked by in high
heels, porters trailing with matching luggage like lost children.
The girls behind the car rental booths all smiled and looked fresh.
You wish you could start with the Avis girl one night and have the
Hertz girl the next, ending with the Budget one for the weekend. I
walked down the long line of ticket counters looking for depar-
tures. At the TWA booth I saw Washington, DC. Standing in line I
felt dirty. I needed a shower and shave and a change of clothes.

When it was my turn in line the male ticket attendant smiled faintly. "Ticket to Washington, DC, on flight 702, leaving here at one AM." I looked at the clock. It was four PM. He punched the computer. I told him cash. "One hundred ninety-eight dollars," he told me. I gave him the money. "Window seat," I said. He punched the computer again, put 13A on the ticket and I told him I needed my bag to clean up and would check it in later. "Fine." He looked at the next face in line and smiled faintly once again. I walked until I found the nearest restroom. It was large and clean with urinals on one side of a divider and sinks on the other, I went to the end and opened my bag. Stripping to the waist I turned the water on, adjusted it, and splashed around like a bird in a bird bath. People coming and going paid me no mind. Washed from the waist up I then took off my trousers and bathed as well as I could. I dried off, put on my last pair of clean levis, clean socks and put my boots back on. Then I shaved, splashed on Old Spice and put on a clean shirt. I combed my hair, checked out a few more wrinkles and then remembered I didn't brush my teeth and would probably drip toothpaste on my clean shirt so I took it off and brushed my teeth. A man in a business suit washing his hands laughed. I drip toothpaste on my shirt all the time. Done with that I packed the dirty clothes up and went back to the TWA counter and stood in line once again to check in my bag. Finished I walked around the airport until I found a bar and went in. Sitting at the bar I ordered a Bloody Mary from the cute pixie-looking bartender. She had on a low cut blouse that was frilled around the bodice. The top of her breasts were light brown from wearing a bikini. If I had been rich I would have asked her to go to Mexico with me for a few weeks. But I was not so I only smiled and dreamed about her naked body for a few moments.

Sitting in the airport bar I felt okay. It was not like a bus station where one can feel down and out. You could have a million dollars but sitting in a bus station you would still feel down and out. Poor and down and out, sitting in an airport you can feel okay. Everybody around me looked prosperous, busy, efficient, a part of the system. You can sit and feel like part of the system. Which is okay for a while, as long as you don't let it go to your head and you become part of the system.

To my surprise the pretty bartender came back, pulled a chair up across from me and sat down. There were no other customers at the bar. I looked into the girl's deep green eyes and tried to keep my eyes from straying to her breasts.

"You don't look like most of those creeps," she scowled. "Another man with a gold watch and a business suit cracking on me today and I swear I'm going to spit."

"I'm a creep," I spoke. "I just don't have a suit."

She looked at me as though I was a bug under a microscope and then her lips parted into a pleasing smile. She commented. "Please don't."

I held out my hand. "I won't. Frank's the name." We shook. I grabbed one quick glance at her breasts.

"Here, I'll buy you a drink," she stated and she bounced off her chair and mixed another Bloody Mary for me only that time in a tall glass with a lime and piece of celery in it. Setting in down in front of me she sat down again. "Where are you headed, Frank?"

"Washington, DC," I answered.

"I would have never guessed that. What in the hell for?"

I looked at the girl. It would have been easy to evade the question but I asked myself why. "I'm going to see the Vietnam Veterans Memorial."

She looked at me and there was no look of shock or pity. "You must be a veteran."

I nodded my head.

"You know," she went on. "I don't know anything about that war."

I laughed feeling relieved. "I don't either." Two men in business suits sat at the end of the bar. She made a face at me and walked over to them. She was not friendly. I wondered what it was about business suits.

As I sipped the free drink I thought about her statement. "I don't know anything about that war." One can get so wrapped up in one's problems, it's easy to forget everybody didn't experience them. "Jesus Christ," I muttered. I wondered what the world would be like if we all had the same problems. We could all sit around and talk about the same things. But then everybody would have to have been born at the same time. The bartender came back and sat down. "They think you are my boyfriend so they didn't say anything."

"Good," I answered. With the drink finished I stood up. I needed to walk around. Sitting on the bus, sitting in the cab, all I had been doing was sitting. "Good luck," I told the girl. She smiled. "I need it."

I walked around the airport and looked at cars on display and paintings for sale on the walls. I looked at children running and people hurrying and ashtrays overflowing with butts. I watched the maintenance man buff a section of the floor and people file out of airplaces like cattle. I went to the observation deck and watched the planes land and take off and watched the sun go down and the lights of the city take over the night. I felt big and filled with life and small and nonexistent at the same time. I bought a small spiral-bound writing pad and a pen at a shop and walked to my gate. It was nine-thirty. I had three and a half hours to wait. The seats were empty. The flight was already posted for departure at one AM. Sitting down I took a deep breath, flipped open the writing pad and began to write:

1. War is another part of life
2. Losing isn't the end
3. Rejection is what you make of it
4. Prison is a bad place
5. Man tries
6. Love is all important

Then I thought of Barbara and I was standing on the corner of LA, feeling lost with her looking at me and saying, "Come with me." I was the cur dog and she was the princess. "Come with me, I feel your need, I see you have a heart. I have scented soap and soft towels and a bed. I'll show you the ocean and take you out to eat and you can sleep with me. You can come into me and empty yourself of your pain and hurt. I will never understand but I will be your vessel. I will be your friend. I will be your lover. I care. For all the mysteries of life, for all the chance meetings, I do not question. I just am. And at this moment, on this corner, I love you Frank. I know I love you."

I thought about the girl at the bus stop and her nakedness in the van. I wondered if Barbara had slept with other men while I had traveled around. I wondered if it had left her empty inside when they laid together afterwards like it had me with my eyes open, my heart yearning, my soul bothered. I wrote once again in my note pad.

7. Making love is not love unless you love.

I looked out through the windows at the runway lights, blue and green and red, and I could see Barbara as she swam in the ocean. She was all that was good and alive. All that was a woman. A start, a reason, a beginning. I saw her laughing when I plunged into the cold water and ran out with goose bumps over my white untanned body and her smile as we walked to her house with me in the bathing suit and cowboy boots. I saw her standing in her bikini, the thin material clinging to the curves of her breasts and womanhood and with me stealing her smile and her eyes. I felt her touch when we made love, bathed in candlelight. Soft touches, the gentleness of her insides, the peace of our thrusts. I felt the warmth of her breasts against my face and the sleep without dreams and when I awoke, her breathing and her heartbeat in my ear. I could stand up and reach out from that airport and bring her to me. Our fingers touched through the veil of night and stars. In my mind I could hear her murmur in my ear. "I am here, it's okay, I am here." And then I was sad. A dark cloud engulfed me. I was sad for the world, sad for the veterans, sad for war and poverty. Sad that nothing was equal, sad for the oppressed, sad for the old men sitting on park benches all over the world, living in the dreams of the past. I was sad for Grace going to sleep in the old house, smelling of time and dust, waiting to die to see her husband. I was sad for the believers and the nonbelievers, the proud and the unproud. I was sad for the young soldiers and I was sad for those who never knew love.

I stood up and walked quickly to a pay phone and dialed Barbara's number. On the second ring she answered and I shut my eyes. "Barbara."

Her voice was soft. "Frank."

"Barbara, for no reason, for nothing practical, I love you. I want you to know that."

"I love you too," she answered. "I love you." I stood listening to her breathing on the phone. It was enough. Words were not necessary. Only the sound of life. "Frank, do what you have to do."

"I am," I answered and I hung up.

I walked away from the phone. Outside I knew the air was filled with poisons. Outside I knew the world was filled with problems and crises and hate and injustice. But at that moment it did not matter. Sitting back down in the gate area I opened up my pad once again and wrote:

8. Life must go on . . . it must

9. Bedrooms— the insides of flowers— bring joy to the heart.

I shut the pad, put the pen in my pocket and watched a sleek jet filled with hopes and dreams of many people climb for the heavens. There were only twenty or thirty people that boarded the plane. I walked through the first-class section. There were three men in pin-stripped suits and a woman who could have been a jewelry store. Second class was like the bus station. We knew we were inferior, rising in the back of the airborne bus. Those up front would drink free but we lower class would dig deep into our pockets for quarters and dimes if we wanted a beer or a cocktail. A curtain was drawn, segregating us from the front of the plane. Poetic justice, that when these birds crash those in the front have the least hope of surviving. Many in the back probably wished they would die. But we glanced at each other and smiled, finding reassurance in our positions of subservience. The stewardess pushing the cart looked fatigued, probably wishing she had seniority and could wait on the first-class pin-strippers with their talk of stocks and bonds and vacations. I would arrive in DC at six AM after a stop in Atlanta without getting off. I drank two beers and felt dizzy. The tired stewardess ignored me as she passed. I had to wave to her to take the empty beer cans and when she did, I knew it was a bother as her eyes looked above my head. Below me buses plied the highways. It was all nothing but a bus ride. Reclining my seat and closing my eyes, my last thought was of a prison guard shocked that somebody would throw him the finger.

I awoke when we landed in Atlanta but fell back asleep and did not wake up again until the plane was taxiing to the gate in Washington. There must have been a stewardess change in Atlanta because the new lady was smiling and cheerful as I walked by. "Thank you for flying TWA," she piped between perfect teeth and beaming eyes. I nodded my head, my mind still fogged from sleep. In the airport life was beginning to take form. On the horizon the sulpher and carbon monoxide air glowed red as people rushed by. I got my bag from the conveyor belt that reminded me of some prehistoric beast ingesting insects and spitting out luggage. With suitcase in hand I located a coffee shop and drank two cups of coffee served to me by a black waitress whose hair was braided into tiny ringlets and whose ears seemed as though they would fall off with the load of ear rings they supported. With the third cup of coffee steaming before me I ordered a sweet roll and ate it slowly, knowing there was no nourishment to sustain me through the day. It was fully light when I left the airport and hailed a taxi. The driver was an Arab of some sort. We did not talk except when I told him, "Take me to the Veteran's Memorial." He nodded his head and we were off. He did not put my suitcase in the trunk. Maybe living in Washington, DC, he expected to be ripped off. I was oblivious to the traffic and the buildings. My usual thought entering my mind was didn't anybody know about birth control. When the cab stopped I looked at the meter and gave him six dollars with no tip. He spun his tires leaving with the early morning. Off to my right, sitting on a knoll, was the monument, a long black ribbon bending and curving with the names of the dead engraved on its face. It flowed like a dream, gyrated like a nightmare. Looking at the black ribbon I felt nervous. My hands grew sticky and my forehead was hot. My heart seemed not to beat and my tongue grew dry and thick in my mouth. I wanted to turn and run away from the ribbon but I stood and then walked slowly towards it.

A man and a woman, looking to be in their fifties, stood holding each other while the woman's finger traced an engraved name. The man did not look strong as the woman cried. Both held onto each other for comfort. There was no stronger or weaker. I set my suitcase down by the A's and began to read. Adams, Andres, Baker, Brown. On and on I read. Charles, Dikers, Emory, Freeman, Granger, Hillerman, Jones. Names, letters one after the other, forming names. Names that were living flesh. Flesh with hearts and souls and wants and desires. Names filled with hope and pride and glory and honor. Names with no blood. Names carved into stone that could not see the memory. I did not feel the tears that ran down my face. I did not feel the snot that covered my lips. I did not see other people or hear the cars or buses. Just names. Sylvester, Towers. I stopped and shut my eyes and rested my head against the honor roll of causes. There were flares in the night sky, there were red tracers searching through the night, demons of death. There were arms and legs shattered around me and the moans of faceless men. There was the noise of helicopters and the thudding of mortars. The cries of the enemy burning only yards away. There were the eyes of children and the tits and cunts of whores smelling like many men with no hope. There were piles of burnt and fractured gooks piled like cordwood, counted like rabbits or quail. And there was the fear and the dark . . . and the dark. And there were faces to some of the names. Smiles and groans. Cigarettes hanging from the lips and sweat pouring from the chest. Faces talking about girls and home. Faces who were friends. Faces who were brothers. Faces that would stay that way forever in my mind. No aging, not decaying, not wrinkling, but remaining young and alive and brave. Brave. Spitting at the fear. Spitting at the hell. Fighting for love. For country. And home. For girls and kids. And dying. Dying to be those letters on that ribbon.

I stepped back from the plaque. A man came up to me and there were tears in his eyes. Without word he handed me a handkerchief and I wiped my face and nose. He walked away, I holding his handkerchief. Down away from the memorial two children ran and played. A lady sat on a bench, her hand in her lap. I looked back towards the beginning of the memorial for my suitcase but it was gone. I walked away. I was not ashamed, I was not guilty because I believed. Inside my back pocket I could feel the outline of the pad of paper I had bought. I sat down on a patch of grass and took it out and wrote:

10. Tears

But nothing else came, only a feeling that a great weight was lifting from my mind. Years melted away and in my heart I could feel a rainbow forming. I walked away not looking back. There was no looking back. There was only tomorrow and the day after that and the day after that and the day after that.

As I walked I felt a gentle tap on my shoulders. It was the lady who was sitting on the bench. Her eyes were dark and distant, her lips drawn. Her auburn hair moved with the wind. "I watched you," she spoke lowering her eyes and then raising them to mine she fell into me and wrapped her arms around my neck. She pulled away gently and I dabbed her eyes with the handkerchief and pushed several strands of hair from her forehead and kissed her on the cheek. We stepped back and smiled at each other and it was okay. Our eyes said it was okay. I turned without speaking and could hear the click of her high heels as she walked in the other direction.

I could hear the words of my grandmother as we sat by the farm pond. "Love lies bleeding." But I knew love might bleed but it did not die. Not as long as a man hung onto hopes and dreams, it did not die. Not as long as one human believed in justice and equality and peace, it did not die.

CHAPTER X

I was sitting in the first-class section of the airplane. My ticket was two hundred-ninety dollars and I had fifteen dollars left to my name. I bought a toothbrush and a small tube of toothpaste in the airport and had brushed my teeth. Brush and tube were sticking out of my shirt pocket. In my back pocket was my note pad and pen sitting comfortably. The stewardess had been cordial but was much more interested in another man who sat across from me with his blue suit and a Rolex watch on his left wrist and a gold bracelet on the right. It was nonstop flight. Lunch was some type of chicken with mixed vegetables and a piece of chocolate cake and coffee. We had flown over mountains and farms, cities and small towns. America from the sky. A conglomerate of people. Each town different from the next. Each geographic area unique in its own way but all tied together under the one word of America. If that plane had continued to fly and fly, it would have passed over the world. All the countries and people and the hopes and dreams. The time was coming when the earth would be just the world. It had to come. Maybe it would come when we had destroyed so much we would have to grow together. Maybe it would come when a huge wave of consciousness swept over the planet. Maybe it would come from divine inspiration. I only knew that it would come. One day it would. It would come when all man knew that all we needed was a home and food and love. When we realized there was no first class or second class. We are all an integral part of each other.

When the plane landed I let all the passengers file by before I left the plane. Inside the airport I walked directly to the outside and waved a cab. The air burned my nose and my eyes watered. The cabby looked for my bags. "Plane lost them," I commented. He shrugged his shoulders. "Happens all the time," he consoled.

When the taxi stopped I gave him ten dollars. I breathed deep the smell of the ocean and walked down the street to the beach. Out on the water a freighter passed silently. Three sailboats skipped across the small wave and two bikini clad girls walked by. I admired their tanned legs and breasts and the motion of their behinds. I saw a face swimming in the ocean, wet bonde hair clinging to it features. Looking at the beach I saw a towel. I walked to it and sat down. The blonde face emerged from the water slowly.

First the neck was exposed, then the shoulders, then the breasts filled with hope and covered by a small strip of white material. Then the bare ribs and the stomach and the small wedge of material that covered the womanhood. The graceful flow of thighs leading to calves and delicate feet. The face grew into a form. Eyes sparkled, lips turned to a smile, the legs filled with life and ran across the sand. The form was on top of me, dripping with ocean water, and my shirt and pants became wet. I fell back on the towel, wet hair falling on my face and lips came to mine. Then we were standing and laughing and the towel was picked up and we walked to the street and up the slight hill and up the stairs to the home. The home with flowers in the windows and soft towels in the bathroom with scented soap in the soap dish and a bedroom that was like the inside of a flower. We were laying on the bed, wet swim suit and clothes on the floor and I was tasting the sea salt taste of bare breast. "Frank," the voice was saying. "You were gone so long. I thought you'd never come back."

I pressed my ear to the beat of her heart and sighed. "I never left you, Barbara. I never left you." I felt her fingers run through my hair and everything was okay . . . everything was okay.

www.ingramcontent.com/pod-product-compliance
Lightning Source LLC
Chambersburg PA
CBHW022140020726
47496CB00008B/2489